COPPER TRANCE & MOTORWAYS

A lawyer and retired local government Chief Executive, Andrew Sparke has reinvented himself as a writer and Indie Publisher. He owns and manages APS Publications, a vehicle for fiction, poetry, food, travel, photography, sport, erotica, music, health and spirituality, publishing other indie authors as well as his own work.

News and much more information is available from the website www.andrewsparke.com

'Copper Trance & Motorways' is the second of his Lincoln trilogy, the first being 'Abuse, Cocaine and Soft Furnishings'. A third entitled 'Anger Limerence & Fault Lines' is in preparation. The novels can be read individually and in any order with some events and characters overlapping in each.

OTHER BOOKS FROM APS PUBLICATIONS

(www.andrewsparke.com)

FICTION

Abuse Cocaine & Soft Furnishings (Andrew Sparke)

Initiation (Pete Sears)

POETRY

Gutter Verse & The Baboon Concerto (Andrew Sparke)

Broken English (Andrew Sparke)

Fractured Time (Andrew Sparke)

Refracted Light (Andrew Sparke)

Silent Melodies (Andrew Sparke)

Vital Nonsense (Andrew Sparke)

Failing To Be Serious (Lee Benson)

Meandering With Intent (Lee Benson)

NON-FICTION:

War Shadows (Andrew Sparke)

Bella In The Wych-Elm (Andrew Sparke)

Rear Gunner (Andrew Sparke)

Piggery Jokery In Tonga (Andrew Sparke)

Stutthof (Andrew Sparke)

Indie Publishing: The Journey Made Easy (Andrew Sparke)

Tithes & Offerings (Rebirtha Hart)

Changing Lives (Keith Horsfall & Andrew Sparke)

Croc Curry & Oil Wells: Surviving Nigeria (Paul Dickinson)

Your Kid And Crohn's: A Parent's Guide (William Sparke)

COPPER TRANCE & MOTORWAYS

Andrew Sparke

Copper Trance & Motorways

©2016 APS Publications

ISBN 9780957621183

Cover photograph from Thinkstock and cover creation by Noxiousdesign

APS Publications, 4 Oakleigh Road, Stourbridge, West Midlands, DY8 2JX

www.andrewsparke.com

CHAPTER I: ONE DAY EARLY JUNE

Not sure where I'm going to be in a moment. Alive or dead. Or suspended somewhere between the two. Adrenalin surging. Brain-cells working overtime to find a way out. Just the hint of a gap in the outside lane to pull into. Trying desperately to escape the violently braking car in front. A dark-coloured hatchback. Noted by an aloof part of my cerebral cortex. If that's where irrelevant detail gets stored. A car which drifts, still braking, back into my path. Braking too hard myself. Something's squealing. My tyres or my mouth. Yanking the steering to get into the space he's vacated in the middle lane. Is it a he? How do I know that? Front wheel-arch clips the stranger's rear nearside. Everything suddenly soggy - unresponsive. Car yawing violently. Wrestle it as it slews through two lines of traffic. The back of a coach looms and is gone. Thank Christ I didn't hit that. Onto the hard shoulder. Still braking. Almost safe. Not absolutely straight though. A front wheel touches the stones separating the safety lane from the grass and it's enough to start the barrel-rolling of my universe. A complete roll up the embankment. And down again at an angle. A second revolution half complete. Ending with my car on its roof. Mostly on the motorway hard shoulder. As near as dammit at ninety degrees to the oncoming traffic. Nose just breaking the demarcation line with the carriageway. No more movement. And at first no sound that I can take in. Just the stench of spilt fuel.

And I'm hanging from my seatbelt, puzzled. Wondering what just happened and what comes next. There's nothing impinging on me at all. No sense of my life having flashed before my eyes. No pain. Nothing but surprise to find myself where I am. Upside down.

Quite calm. The only thought in my head, *Thank God. I get to go home alive.* Then. *Shit. I've got to go home again*! Reach out and turn off the ignition. Not a planned action. Just an instinctive thing to do. Find the door-handle doesn't work. Skew my body around so I can kick it with both feet. It opens with a horrible scraping noise. Release the seat-belt catch and let myself slide down onto the ceiling. Crawl out. Stand up. Knees should be jellified. But they're not. Bend down and completely irrationally

1

wriggle back into the car to retrieve my book and my glasses. Back out and onto my feet. Walk round the inverted vehicle. The wheels have stopped spinning. They look so odd, silhouetted against a grey sky. And one of them has only shreds of rubber where a tyre used to be.

Sit down on the grass and wait.

Normal hearing begins to return. After a fashion. But still feel I'm in a different world to everybody else. Despite everything happening around me. Traffic roaring past. The stationary coach a bit further up the motorway. Glad I missed colliding with that. People getting out now. Running towards me. Shouting. What's that about? Can't take it in.

A woman says she's a nurse. Touches me carefully and methodically. Feeling my head and moving my limbs about. Let her if she wants to.

A man in a suit suddenly there, pulling out a mobile phone and making a call. Who wears a suit and tie on a Saturday afternoon for God's sake?

He says, "Was it that dark Ford Focus? He overtook me driving like a dickhead just before he hit you."

Think I hit him actually. When he pulled in front of me and braked. He had no reason to do that. What was he doing? Was it a man at all? Don't know. Don't care.

Something at the periphery of vision catches my eye. Look up. The flashing blue and whites of a police car coming up the hard shoulder. Stopping a few yards short of my overturned Citroen. The first to reach them as they get out is the smartly-dressed man with the mobile phone. Whatever he says to them seems to help. They're smiling as they walk across to me. One of them is taller. Close-cropped head lending him a hard edge. The other older, darker. In his thirties. Welsh-looking. If I'm allowed to say that. Or is my incipient racism leaking out?

The senior presence says, "Are you hurt, sir?" No trace of a discernible accent at all. Not a Taffy then.

2

"Yes. I think so."

"You're bleeding sir." His partner touches a finger to my forehead. He's wearing latex gloves now. I didn't even notice him snapping them on.

"No. It's not my head. Just my finger. Cut it when I went back into the car to get the book I was reading. I don't mean I was reading when I was driving..." There's a whole load of broken glass from the side window. The windscreen's still intact. In one piece despite all the radiating cracks criss-crossing over it.

"Can you stand up?"

"Yes."

"Come and sit in the car with me." He puts me in the front passenger seat. He leaves the door ajar. It's a warm evening. Presumably he doesn't think I'm about to abscond. Goes round to the other side and gets in behind the wheel. Takes out a notebook. Asks me what happened. Tell him about the lunatic driver. He asks my registration number and to see my driving licence. Calls my details in on his radio. Comments on my birthdate. "I'd've guessed a bit older."

"I look after myself. Don't smoke. And don't drink much."

Recipe for a long life. Shame there's a phenomenon known as risk substitution. Instead of abusing my body with nicotine and alcohol, I drive too fast.

"You said you clipped the Ford?"

"I must have. Think that's when my tyre burst."

"He didn't stop". News to me. "There aren't any cameras on this stretch so unless someone on the coach got his licence plate, we've no way to catch him. You were very lucky..." His final thought. "He was probably on drugs".

Does his paperwork, while his mate puts some cones out and talks to potential witnesses and I sit there.

Eventually asks if I belong to a motoring organisation.

Shrug. "The AA."

He calls for a breakdown vehicle. The coach sets off again. Wait some more. The tow-truck arrives. Just one man in it. Pulls past and then backs up to my poor car. Hooks a cable onto the door pillar. Gets in. Drives a few yards. Enough traction to pull the car over so it's the right way up. Re-attaches the cable to the front axle. And winches the whole thing onto the truck-bed. The whole job takes perhaps ten minutes.

My cop says "Go and sit in the cab. He'll be off in a minute. He'll take you back to his garage and they can sort things out from there. Go carefully now".

Which makes me smile. Of course I bloody will.

The garage man starts to talk as soon as he's underway. Tells me what a day he's already had. "Worst was a two car head-on. Both dead. Right mess. Got a concertinaed BMW in the yard and a Mini-Cooper that's just bits. "How did you do yours?"

Start to tell him and a thought occurs to me. They didn't even bother to breathalyse me.

CHAPTER II: JUNE TO MARCH

Nothing like a near-death experience to make you face up to the truth. And the truth? Life sucks. Not all of it obviously. Just the big stuff; marriage, job and the prospects of much changing without a colossal push.

Sitting in a High Street coffee shop, drinking double espresso with plenty of sugar. Sipping it. Making it last. A few feet away from me a neatly made-up young woman sits beside a much older man. Him: horn-rimmed glasses and fawn fleece top. Over-sixties wear from the gents outfitters two doors up. Her: dark business suit and sensible shoes. Cups of tea and a shared Daily Mail rest on the table before them.

He says "See that woman selling 'New Look' over there..."

"It's 'Big Issue', Dad."

"Close enough."

"Not remotely."

Tune them out.

Decisions are edging around the corner of my brain. The fog of emotion from the accident beginning to lift. Leaving several crystal-clear thoughts in place. This life can end tomorrow. You don't know when it's going to be over. Saturday could have been the end. And it wasn't. Why wasn't it? And I'm miserable. Not even vaguely content. What the hell am I going to do about it? The car's already gone. What's to stop me writing off the rest? Nothing of course. Except lack of courage.

And suddenly it's a done deal. This has been coming for a very long time. Absolutely certain what I have to do. Just the tricky stuff now. Implementation. Ditch the mournful marriage which drives me into working every hour God sends and find a new job. Somewhere else entirely. Easy then!

***

At least my timing's lucky. A glut of senior public sector vacancies up and down the country and a paucity of experienced candidates. So a decent opportunity leaps out at me from the pages of the Local Government Chronicle. A post where I'd be the boss and could make whatever I want out of a new challenge. And get out of this dirty cesspool of a city. Move to Lincoln. Where nobody knows me. To start again. Falling on my feet.

***

Walk through the sliding glass doors into the reception area. The low desk ahead is staffed by two smartly turned out girls in navy-blue jackets. To my left there's a tall woman. Red-haired. Not that brassy bottle red colour. Her mane is flecked with all the golden-orange of living flame. You couldn't replicate the complexity of it with highlights if you spent a month on it. What a colour! And to cap it all she's got a cone in her hand. It's October for God's sake. Why's she licking ice-cream? Her tongue laps at it with an enthusiasm bordering on the erotic. Much too close to suggestive in fact. Shouldn't be allowed. She catches my eye and grins. Hurry past her to the desk at the risk of losing all composure. And making a poor first impression where it really matters. With my new staff.

Say who I am and wait for my newly inherited personal assistant to come down and collect me.

"Hello. Remember me? I'm Jane Roberts." Turn to smile and shake hands with an older woman, the highly competent blonde who supervised all the interviewees for the job I've won. A matter of a few weeks ago. Imperceptibly slide into feeling relaxed and comfortable. She's done that with both grace and charm. It's going to be fine. As first days go.

***

A new routine is quickly established; the leader of the council, Neil Wetton, popping in to see me early most mornings and then Jane and I falling into the habit of morning coffee together, while going through the diarised meetings. Create my checklist for the day. All the things I'd like to clear but probably won't. Sometimes cheat and start with tasks already virtually completed. Crossing them straight out again gets the day off to a flying start. Psychologically good for the soul.

A few days in and it's..."Councillor Ross wants to see you. Have you met him yet?"

"Only at the council meeting when they confirmed my appointment. What's he like, Jane?"

"You probably already know he's the former leader." I don't know that at all but it's good of her to pretend I might. "Not the last one. The one before that. Bit of a maverick but a nice man. And a very proud Yorkshire-man."

"Let's have a look at the diary then. I'd better squeeze him in."

"Okay. I'll ring him and say it's a yes."

In the meantime there's all the other stuff Jane allows into my schedule. Such as a deputation from the oriental community's leading citizens. The Yungs and their acolytes. Wanting more council facilities for next Chinese New Year. Thinking well in advance. Like that. Suspect we can help them too.

The steady procession of visitors continues all week as it doubtless will every week. Staff, supplicants and complainants, some justified, others grossly unreasonable.

And then, of course, the politicians. Life with the lions. Or the hyenas. There was a jackal-headed God in Egyptian mythology wasn't there? Anubis if memory serves correctly. A few of my political jackals seem to suffer from belief in their own divinity. And they wonder why there's such an obvious disconnect between the general public and their underworld. Whichever party they claim to represent today. Cynical? Me? When it comes to councillors and members of parliament; guilty as charged. But they pay my wages. And there are honourable exceptions. Like the former leader perhaps.

Peter Ross is everything Jane said and more. A bluff Northerner. Outgoing and direct to the point of rudeness. But underneath the gruff exterior, a good heart.

"Well, young man. About time you got to know to me. I won't be troubling you unless it's important or something's really bothering me."

"That's good then. For my part if there's anything you ought to hear about from me, I promise you will."

"So we understand each other. The favour I wanted to is if you to see someone for me. He's got a story you need to hear. And he's my son-in-law." Corrects himself. "Ex-son-in-law. Don't think he'll be wasting your time either."

"Then of course I'll meet him. Let's have Jane put it in the book."

"Thank you. That's it then."

"Good to see you."

"Likewise. And best of luck with the job."

"Thanks Peter." I've already resolved to put all new relationships on first name terms. Never show subservience to politicians. It excites their worst instincts.

***

Being geographically remote from the problems of ending a marriage doesn't solve anything of course. The wonder of modern tele-communications sees to that. Jane gently handles or deters too many interruptions into the working day from my former nearest and dearest, letting Marianne through the net only when things are quiet or she judges me to be in the right mood to handle confrontation. But there are still too many calls from London and too many arguments. Getting divorced doesn't seem like it's going to be either consensual or particularly straightforward. Going to need a decent lawyer.

Nor does granting a meeting to a councillor's former son-in-law turn out to be such a pleasure after all. What he places on my desk sounds unmistakeably like a softly disguised allegation of corruption. Something which won't stay brushed under the carpet. Nor should it. The runes don't read well. Undervalued sites and unmerited planning consents. The stuff of probable sleepless nights to come.

It's time to test who I can rely on. See where the real loyalties of this place lie. Starting with Jane. If I can't trust her then this job's untenable at every level. Check through workload issues and all the other stuff I need her to take care of for me before broaching what's really on my mind.

"I've been landed with a major headache. I'm going to need help and I'll be straight with you. This could be a sticky mess which nobody thanks us for opening up. I need to know I have your absolute discretion. I can't afford to have anything leaking to anybody. That includes members. If we find a prima facie case, this is going straight to the police. Okay?"

Jane looks slightly affronted that I should have to ask but says she understands. "What do you need me to do?"

"How long have you been with the council?"

"Twelve years."

"So you know most of the officers."

"Yes." A smug little smile.

"Let's start by going through the internal directory and working out where the problem areas could be. And I'll also need someone to brief me in more detail on the football club. Who looks after our stake in that?"

"Economic Development. The team leader's John Howard. Not been here that long. Came from Sheffield City Council. Already pretty well regarded. He's already got a slot in your diary early next week. Wants to bend your ear about one of his pet projects around industrial starter units. Do you need to see him earlier than that?"

"No. That's good. Just pre-warn him I'll need to get up to speed on the City Ground after we've looked at the big strategic issues."

"I'll do that. And it's called Sincil Bank. That's the street it's on."

"Thank you. Do I get a coffee now?"

Jane laughs. "Of course you do. And can I say one thing?"

"What's that?"

"This is already more exciting than anything in the last few years."

"Then you've led a sheltered life. And I don't want too much excitement, thank you."

"Speak for yourself." Not sure she's kidding. But I think she's already proven herself one of the good'uns.

So not bad for my first month. Lots of novelty and not much to dread. Wish the same was true of my Saturday trips back down to the smoke to see Marianne to discuss resolving our situation. At her insistence. I'd happily give seeing her a miss but it's probably better to go, given the increasing number of phone calls Jane has to field from her every week.

***

The issue I've been saddled with by Peter Ross, should be factually straightforward. Wish it was. Turn over a stone in anything in which money can be made illegally and what emerges into the light is always worse than you imagined. And then there are my underlying concerns. There's a worrying element of blatancy. Indicative of deep-seated problems.

Get the file together. Call the city commander, Chief Superintendent Clare James.

"Welcome to Lincoln." She sounds bright and efficient, so far as one can tell from a voice on the phone. "What can I do for you on this beautiful morning?"

"Can we meet? Unfortunately I've already got a matter I need to run past you."

"Okay. Your place or mine?"

"Which would you prefer?"

"The tea's better at yours. Need to send my current support officer over for lessons. Tomorrow afternoon any good?"

"Works for me." Agree a time. "Thanks."

***

Clare James. Not exactly pretty. Striking would be a more accurate description. It's in the way she carries herself. Upright. Proud. Smart. Sexy. Shouldn't say that of a police officer of course. But she is. She takes the promised cup of tea, palms herself a custard cream from the proffered plate of biscuits on the coffee table, settles back onto one of my comfortable chairs, picks up the file I nudge across to her and starts reading. After a few minutes she says something exceptionally welcome. "You can leave this to me. It fits into an ongoing investigation. Local shark called Lenahan. I can sort this out. We'll need to formally interview some of your people in due course but..."

"And I'll need to manage the public relations consequences when you do that. If you can let me know quickly if any councillors are implicated, I can cut them out of the loop. Especially if any of the leadership's involved."

"Be careful of the Chair of Planning. But it won't be your leader. He's straight as a die. I'd brief him now if you want my advice."

"Thanks. I will."

Clare drains her tea and gets to her feet, retrieving her uniform cap, the file and her mobile from the table.

"Good luck with the job."

"Why does everybody assume I need luck? Do you all know something I don't?"

"Probably not. It'll be good working with you."

"Likewise. Just one thing. What does one do for entertainment in this city?"

"Do you like live music? Plenty of that. Even if you exclude the student scene. Nice pubs and restaurants. And Nottingham's just down the road. Where are you living?"

"I'm thinking of buying a place in the West End."

"Well, give me a shout then and I'll introduce you to The Queen in the West."

"That'd be nice. Thank you."

"Be good."

"I'll try."

Breezes out, leaving a sense of anti-climax behind her. Sigh. Have another biscuit. Take up the next file.

***

They've put me up at the Eastgate Hotel. An anonymous concrete block to the north of the cathedral. Comfortable enough. Probably worth its stars. Just lacking in character. But then again, don't most modern hotels? Won't stay here longer than necessary. Need to find that house I can rent or buy. Start looking. Late Victorian terraces. Well-proportioned. Names reflecting their era. Like Colenso Terrace with its Boer War associations. Five minutes' walk to work. Perfect location.

Organise a survey for a three-bedroomed house needing some work, but nothing too extensive. Fun to do up and a good precaution against spending too much of my life in the office. And could make some money on it longer term. Jane recommends local solicitors, MacFarlane & Co. Go and see Patrick Butler. A bustling little man with half-moon glasses and reedy red hair. Friendly. Helpful.

"If it's a short chain then with a fair wind etcetera, we'll have you in by Christmas, with any luck."

"That would be great. Need to put you in funds. How much do you want upfront?"

"We'll need the 10% deposit before exchange of contracts. You've paid the mortgage fees already? Yes? And I presume my bill..."

"Goes straight to the council. Part of my relocation package."

"Easy then. Forward the mortgage offer on to me when it arrives and we'll take it from there."

"Thank you."

"Welcome to Lincoln. You'll like it here. It's a good city."

"I know that already. Can't wait to get settled."

"Leave it to me then. Anything else I can help you with?

"Well...there might be. Do you do matrimonial work?"

"Nah. But I know a man who does. Let me find you his card."

***

What should I say about my wife? If you met her you'd see a soft-natured and bright brunette. That's how she presents. Discovering her temper and obstinate streak takes time. Or perhaps those traits materialised only post-marriage. In which case I may have provided the necessary triggers.

She starts as predicted. "Is there someone else?" An automatic assumption whenever a relationship's gone off the rails.

I could counter-attack. The hours I work, when would I have the time? But I keep it simple. And truthful. And non-confrontational.

"No."

Marianne starts to cry. It's an act. Something she can do at will. She knows I can't bear her tears. Would do almost anything to stop them. Not this time. I've grown out of responding as she wants me to. Can't afford surrender. Not with the rest of my life at stake. Hand her the box of tissues from the side-board. Need to stand aloof. Above all else, don't fall into the trap of offering physical comfort in any form whatsoever. No arm round the shoulder. No hand-holding. Don't show weakness. Do not under any circumstances give in.

"What's going to happen to me? How will I manage financially, physically, emotionally?" Interesting the order in which she chooses to marshal those concepts.

"Nothing that dreadful. You've got a good income in your own right. Even if we put the house on the market now, it'll take a while to sell and we'll find you something else. Closer to your family if you want. We've got significant equity to share. You'll be okay."

"So you say..." The unspoken accusation that she cares and I don't. She's right.

"You'll be fine in every way. Really you will. You're not telling me you've been happy with the way things have been between us. Are you?"

"No. But I thought you'd come round and things would get better again."

"But even before I left, we were hardly in each other's lives anymore. We didn't go anywhere together. Didn't do anything. You spent way more time with your sister and her kids than you ever did with me."

Tactical mistake mentioning children. Brings about a reversion to sob tactics. "I thought we'd have our own family."

Which is when I start to get tough on her. "It's hard to have children when you don't even sleep together." Realise she'll take that as personal criticism. Me blaming her. Which wouldn't be fair. Have to accept that responsibility. "And that's my fault. Not yours."

Fault? Is not fancying somebody a matter of fault? Or just an unfortunate facet of increasing incompatibility?

Anyway her mood changes as sharply as a click of the fingers. Her slap rocks my head and leaves a reddening print across my cheek. Grab her wrists and let her exhaust her rage. Until I deem it safe to release her. She stands and heads upstairs. Her next utterance aimed over her departing shoulder at me hints encouragingly at burgeoning hatred. "You're pathetic! I want your stuff gone."

It's not her last word on the matter, of course, and find I'm loading clothes, books and other possessions into my car amid a flurry of recriminations and threats. "Don't think I'm agreeing to divorce you unless you give me the house."

Money again. It's always money with some women. I'm so tired of it. I want passion and companionship. And a bit of peace would be nice. Snatch up the old guitar I never learned to play but still love owning. When I go to say "Goodbye", she's sitting dumbly in the lounge and doesn't respond. Exhausted by confrontation. Me too. Close the front door gently behind me. I'm definitely doing the right thing. The relief is intense.

Go back to Lincoln and mull things over while I polish my shoes. One of my favourite chores. Making them gleam. An art form practised with dusters, brushes and spit.

***

So the divorce is going to be problematic, but at least the job is panning out. If I close my mind to the belief that one or two of my newly inherited staff may be corrupt. In my experience the worst as well as the best elements of any public sector position are always about people. They can delight you but just as easily screw up your working life.

Very quickly I get to see and do some pretty amazing things. Dinner in the inner chamber of The Guildhall with visiting celebrities and minor royalty. Ceremonial occasions at the cathedral with chapter members and their wives; the Dean, Sub-Dean and Praecentor. Glad-handing ministers and members of parliament. Tours of local businesses and even a brewery. Good job we're chauffeur driven that day.

An early highlight, thanks to local links with the Air Force, is a trip out of RAF Waddington on a so-called Sentry. A big Boeing carrying a ten-ton, mushroom-like structure on its back. Part of the UK's early-warning system, watching for missile and other incursions coming over the horizon. Instead of an overview of Lincoln, the mayor and I get shipped across the North Sea to Denmark and watch enthralled from the cockpit at amazingly close quarters as a huge tanker aircraft sits above us, passing down fuel in mid-air through a swaying, pitching hose. Then returning to base to practice circuits and bumps, which in an aircraft of such size is quite an experience; touch-down and without braking, fire up the engines to take off again. And then do it again and again until the pilot's flying log-book carries all the new entries he requires.

And through all of what outsiders might perceive as junkets, my ongoing focus is on the management of not merely a council but also a major business; one of a handful of bigger employers in a city where small enterprises are the norm.

In my experience though, it doesn't matter what an organisation is or does. There are always staff who choose to stay late and those who bunk off early. Those who seem to give their heart and soul and those who don't. And those who sacrifice far too much of themselves; who should go home at a reasonable hour once in a while and seldom do. It's my job to look more closely. To find the ones who commit to excellence, even if only from nine to five. And those who waste the hours but are always there to be seen, gaining respect for nothing more productive than mere presence. And I have to ensure we change things for the better because this is a council in transition; adapting to new government priorities and fiscal constraint; a time of pay freezes in which the staff need to be coerced and led to respond without an excess of either cynicism or despair. Which they seem to be doing. And yet, my suspicion is of an undercurrent of something smelling none too sweet. The Lenahan case is only the first unwelcome inkling that, deep-down, the barrel may contain an unfair share of rotten apples.

The most immediately puzzling phenomenon is, of all things, a stolen fire surround.

***

Coming back to my office after a brisk sandwich on the run. The outer office door is ajar and Jane's not at her desk. Instead standing in front of it is a woman I've seen before. Copper-coloured hair, worn long. Tall and slim. Bit older than I'd thought on the day I started at City Hall. But not enough to change my first instinctive response to her.

"Hello. Am I expecting you?"

"I'm in your diary. I'm Janice Valency. Councillor Valency." I'm showing some degree of ongoing bafflement when she adds to the description. "County Councillor."

"Aha. You're one of them."

"I am indeed."

Check the open book on Jane's desk. Find the notation which rings a vague bell. "A fireplace?"

"Indeed. A missing fireplace."

"Come in and when Jane's back we'll sort out some tea. Unless you'd rather have coffee."

"No, tea will do just fine."

Lead the way into my inner sanctum. Settle her at the table. "I've met you before, you know."

"Have you? I don't think so."

"My first day here. Early in October. You were standing in the foyer first thing in the morning. With an ice-cream."

She shakes her head. "Not me. I'm diabetic. I don't do ice-cream."

"I'm very sorry then. I must be mistaken. What is it?" She's chuckling - enjoying keeping something to herself.

"Did you think she looked like me then? The ice-cream eater."

"Yes. I did."

"You mean, she was tall with red hair?"

"Exactly."

"That's flattering. You've met my cousin, Alicia. They say we could be sisters. Can't see it myself - beyond superficial first impressions. A few years between us and plenty of differences."

"You share a smile at least."

"Do we?"

"What does Alicia do then?"

"Works for you." Laughs at my surprise. "In the broader sense of the term. She's a City Council employee. A quantity surveyor in your technical division."

"Really? I've not met her in the office yet. Not so far."

"You might need to expedite that pleasure when you hear what I've got to say."

"Okay. Where do you want to start?"

It seems she wants to open up the topic of council houses. "The smarter ones. You've got several."

"Not that I've noticed."

"Well you have. Not on the estates. Odd ones bought for non-materialising road schemes or left to the council in some poor fool's will. Isolated acquired properties. Anyway there's one next door to me. Up off the Bail, near the cathedral."

"Nice area."

"Very. This one was rented to a sweet old couple. They were there years. Quiet. Good neighbours. Tom died a few months back and his wife couldn't look after herself. She went into a home. One of ours. The County's. I helped get her in there. Anyway, then your lot turned up to renovate the house. And they took out a load of fittings."

"Including this fireplace of yours?"

"It's not mine. It's yours. And it's not just any old mantelpiece. It's a very old one by a contemporary of Adams. I've got the same sort in my house. It's worth thousands. I saw them carrying it out in sections. They wrapped it up and put it in the van."

"Who did?"

"Your workmen."

"Alright. What happened next?"

"I thought it was odd, so I tackled the supervisor before the gang left. He said it was part of the refurb and it would probably end up in one of the civic buildings. I phoned Alicia and got her to check the instructions for the property. They were very specifically told to leave all the historic features in situ."

"So this is incompetence? Failing to follow instructions?" Say it hopefully.

"No. It's theft!" Let's that sink in before she adds "You won't ever see that fireplace again. It's not the first time either. A whole ruined Roman fountain came out of the old town a couple of years ago. Supposedly went into store but it just plain disappeared."

"Would you recognise the workmen again?"

"Yes."

"Would you be willing to go round the depot at the end of the day shift and point them out?"

"I could do that. But we may not need to. I took a picture of the van with my mobile. I've got the registration number."

"Superb." Full of admiration for her presence of mind. "Let's see if Jane's back and we'll have that cup of tea. Then I'll need you to go over this again with one of my lawyers."

My brilliant assistant is once more behind her desk. "Tea for three please, Jane. And can you get Ian Porterfield to join us? If he's not around then find Rachel or Tim. Thanks."

A few minutes later and my Head of Legal Services is on the case. And that means it's in very good hands. Can safely leave it to him now. I've got to have a planned hour off to go into town. Rather than spend more time on fireplaces. Unfortunately.

***

Personal time for a fixed fee initial interview lined up with the family law expert recommended by Patrick Butler. A handsome Irishman, not too many years out of law school.

"You're looking for a divorce?"

"Yeah."

"Then we need to identify the grounds."

"I thought divorce was no-fault these days."

"Up to a point it is. But the basis on which a decree nisi can be granted is limited. Perhaps grounds is the wrong word. Except legally. In plain English calling it the circumstances would be more accurate."

"So what are the acceptable...circumstances?"

"Two years separation if the other party gives their consent."

"And if they don't?"

"Then it's five years."

"Long time to wait. We've not been separated five minutes. What else?"

"Adultery."

"By my wife? Not that I know of."

"Then there's unreasonable behaviour. I mean hers of course. That's an area we could work on. All sorts of relationship issues give rise to what could be construed as unreasonable behaviour."

"But she could contest the allegations?"

"She could if she wants to make life difficult. Which gets messy."

"And expensive."

"Well I don't mind that so much. But you might. Your best bet could be to talk her into divorcing you, if you're comfortable with being labelled unreasonable."

"Well, I want to be divorced. If that's unreasonable."

"Precisely. So taking the blame may be the only tactic that'll work."

"Then I'll have to sit down with Marianne again and see what we can work out. What about the financial side?"

"How long were you married?"

"Not so long. A little over six years."

"Any children?"

"No."

"Does your wife work?"

"She's a solicitor."

Laughs. "That's good. Or not so good. What's her specialism?"

"Commercial conveyancing. Mainly."

"Okay. And she doesn't earn as much as you do?"

"No. But she's a junior partner in the company. Her prospects are good."

"To summarise then. Short marriage and no children. Both in employment. We can make a case for a straight fifty-fifty split of your assets. You own a house together?"

"Yes. Couple of hundred grand in equity."

Savings?"

"A bit. Enough to settle our credit cards and maybe pay the lawyers."

"That's important."

"You made that clear already."

"So talk to her sensibly if you can. Try and make it simple. And get her to divorce you, because you're such an unreasonable, selfish bastard."

"Do you describe your other clients that way?"

"All the time, my friend. Occasionally it's even true."

"Thanks very much. So I come back to you when I know where we're going."

"Right. You do that. And we'll sort you out."

Handshakes and goodbyes. Clear advice. No unpleasant aftertaste. Suspect in the months to come I'll definitely be doing more business with Michael O'Suillibhain and his softly appealing accent. If I can get Marianne to see sense. More circuitous talks to look forward to obviously.

***

Sometimes I idly used to wonder just what I'm actually doing with my life. My grandfather used to say that you're put on this earth to enhance it and if you can't do that, you should bugger off. I can't always see where the enhancement bit comes from. Such doubts have been afflicting me significantly more and more since the accident. Then something happens and the self-analysis becomes irrelevant. Things make sense in ways they didn't before and you can convince yourself that you're on the right track. The moment Alicia strolls into my office is definitely one of those times.

She brings for me the static shock of the inevitable. Unfortunately seconds later there's a painful after-shock of futility. She's out of bounds. Nothing is possible with her. Not with a member of staff. Not if I want to stay in this job. Inside a volley of curses starts to flow silently. Mustn't let that show.

"You wanted to see me?"

Catch my breath. "I did. Come and sit down. Here at the table." Move over from my desk to join her. Offer the ubiquitous cup of tea. It's refused. Politely.

"Did your cousin tell you she'd been in to see me?"

"To tell you about the fireplace?"

"Yes."

"She did. What can I add?"

Not going to tell her the unvarnished truth. Which is that there's probably not a lot I need from her. And that the reason for my summons is to satisfy my own curiosity. About her.

"Take me through the check you made on the refurbishment instructions."

Listen to her voice. Sink into its melodic tonality. Almost miss the fact that she's finished talking, and is looking at me quizzically.

"Okay thanks for that. Go and see Ian Porterfield and put it all in a statement. The sooner this is sorted the better."

Attempted gravitas folds too easily when she smiles.

"Will do, boss."

Try not to let her see she's got to me. Just indicate dismissal with a hand. Don't trust myself to speak.

***

Don't get into the house for Christmas. The chain falls apart during the bustling week of the German Christmas Market. No black marks for Patrick Butler. Not his fault. But he leaves me a problem. In the absence of any family escape plans, the new place was to have been my Christmas refuge. Staying through the holiday in The Eastgate Hotel holds no appeal at all. And it's a bit late for an alternative. In the end settle, not too reluctantly, for a week in Dubai. Plenty of sun. No alcohol to speak of which does no harm. Minimal seasonal reminders. A well-equipped gym associated with the hotel. Running a few kilometres each morning before it gets too warm. Until my knees start to protest and that puts an end to jogging for either fitness or pleasure. Lazing by the pool, catching up on my reading. Get through a small stack of novels.

Return to Lincoln suntanned and feeling really rested with New Year behind me. Not sure that will survive re-engaging on the stuff of council modernisation and the finding of stolen fireplaces. Should either prove remotely possible.

Late January and the chain's mended. Contracts are signed and I'll be able to move into my new home in another month or so if my luck holds, as Patrick Butler would say. See the young woman with the red hair a few times. Around and about. Heading in or out of City Hall. Or in the town. Know her name now perfectly well. But if I don't acknowledge that to myself, then I can feign complete disinterest in her. Or anyone else. Once bitten and all that crap.

***

There are plenty of things to keep Chief Executives fretfully awake at night. Find I'm stuck considering number one in an unlimited edition. And I'm not referring to the risk of falling for the hired help. I'm talking about balancing the budget. Particularly difficult for a lawyer with the obvious preference for words over figures. Numbers and sequences don't lodge readily in my head. Not access codes. Nor telephone numbers. And certainly not items on a balance sheet. Give me a verbal reasoning test and I'll score as near perfect as damn it. But a maths test? Fifty percent on a good day. And yet, unlike many accountants of my acquaintance, I can add up, something they seem to regard as the province of mere book-keepers. So I'll struggle through my treasurer's explanations and tables until I've got something useful to question or add. And then I'll take my throbbing head home, thankful it's not a committee night. Actually better than that, it's Friday night and Clare's taking me to the pub.

***

The Queen in the West is just a pub. Nothing more or less. Not too basic. Not too pretentious. It's comfortable. Slightly shabby but that's not true of the beer. Offer to buy the drinks and Clare surprises me by asking for a pint of lager. Perhaps with her it's the legacy of having to out-think and out-drink all her male peers to get to the rank she holds today. Or perhaps she just likes lager.

Find seats in a corner and sup away while Clare lets me in on how Lincoln's really run. An insider's perspective. Realise my attention's drifting, my eye caught by a pretty girl sitting across the room. Too young for me. Re-focus.

Clare's saying "You need to watch out for him. He's a poisonous little toad of a man."

"Sorry. Who...?"

She names an MP whose own parliamentary constituency obviously doesn't provide enough distraction for all his energy. "He thinks because one of the houses he owns is within a couple of miles, that he's got a right to poke his oar in about anything and everything that happens in the city of which he personally disapproves or dislikes. You will get letters from him regularly. Betcha."

"Not had one so far."

"Just you wait. They'll come. Only a matter of time."

So I'm enjoying examining life through the thick glass bottom of a nearly empty glass when someone appears at my elbow. And says "Hi folks."

Look up to find it's Patrick.

Clare wastes no time in giving him his marching orders. "Carling for me and a pint of Old Frogspawn or whatever the guest beer is for him. There's no queue at the bar. Your timing's perfect".

"You know my solicitor then?"

A flicker of a smile. Almost secretive. "You could say that."

Clare's refilled glass appears on the table. Delivered, with a smile from Patrick. "Don't believe half what she says, especially about me, and you won't go far wrong." He moves away to await the other pints.

Weigh up the options and ask her the safer of the obvious questions. "Does he handle your legal problems too?"

"No. We go way back. His family were our next door neighbours when we were growing up. I've known him all my life."

Take my life in my hands to explore the alternative tack. "And it goes further than that now? You don't have to answer that."

"I've been tempted from time to time."

"Say no more. He's coming back."

"He knows how it is anyway. Not that it stops him trying it on."

"I rather gather he's pretty stubborn. And effective at getting things done."

Patrick chips in. "Who is?"

"Who do you think?" Clare's response is lightning quick.

"You're taking my name in vain. Yet again."

"Then your ears should be burning, darling."

The banter continues. Oddly, it almost feels like they're doing it for my benefit. So I can't say I feel excluded at all. Stretch my legs out comfortably underneath the table and hold on for the right moment to intervene. Don't need to. Patrick suddenly changes the subject. "How's the new home? Are you going to have a party? A house-warming's obligatory in these parts."

"I don't know anybody much yet."

"You know us."

"Yes..."

"So a party's a must. And there's something else I've been meaning to suggest. The team. Don't you think that's a good idea, Clare?" He gets the nod and continues as though he never really needed her approval in the first place. "We have a quiz team." He names another pub I haven't found yet. "Tuesday nights. Teams are supposed to be up to six people. We've got five regulars but sometimes Clare or I have to duck out at short notice if work gets in the way. Actually it's usually Clare more than me. Which gets us down to four and scratting around for last minute substitutes. You've got good general knowledge. Sure you must have, so I think you should join us. What do you say?"

Check across with Clare. Another encouraging nod from her. "Then I'll say yes. And thanks very much."

"Next Tuesday then at 7.30. Unless you've got a council meeting. In which case give me a shout to let me know."

"It's a clear evening as far as I know."

"That's a deal then. Drink up. Clare's round."

And so it is.

***

And everything's all right. I've made a hell of a transition. I may have failed to get a trouble-free divorce but I've managed not to be unemployed for more than a couple of weeks and I've bought a house to turn into a home. And I've landed a seat in a pub quiz team. A new life's starting and so I'm sorted. Aren't I?

CHAPTER III: MARCH TO MAY

A little alleyway runs from Hampton Street into the back end of the cul-de-sac called Colenso Terrace. It's a handy shortcut when you've chosen to walk instead of driving into town. Walking along it today, arms laden with bags of foodstuff, affords me a vision of others hard at work. The two people atop a flat-roofed bay are removing a rotten set of first floor sash windows, with a mixture of exasperated gusto and brute force. One of them, hammer in hand, dirty tank top over jeans, sweat running off her, has a mane of red hair, tied back with a green scarf. I can't fail to recognise her. Even from behind. Especially from behind.

"Working hard?"

She doesn't turn or pause to think. "Come to help?"

"You're joking, Alicia."

Now she looks around. Grinning down at me. "Of course. Can't see the boss doing menial labour. 'Scuse me if I don't stop. Got to get the new window in before we lose the light."

"I was serious though. You need a hand?"

Now her smile slips. She looks me up and down. Takes in my expensive leather jacket. "Not in those clothes."

"I'll go and change."

"Really? Where do you live?"

"A few doors up. On Cambridge Drive. Bought it a couple of months ago."

"Okay then. Thanks. You've got five minutes." Such delicious cheek. "And this is Darryl, by the way."

"Hi, Darryl."

The young man in the sagging jeans with the thick mop of blonde hair wipes his brow, muttering an unintelligible greeting of sorts. Obviously a fellow of few words. But I've just gained something productive to do on a Saturday afternoon. Pull on a pair of old camouflage combats and ragged jumper over a heavy metal t-shirt and return to join the fray.

Alicia flashes her widest smile when she sees me climbing the ladder. "Welcome back, soldier. Come and grab one end of this."

Grabbing actually seems to mean heaving until the wood surround gives way and the whole side of the wrecked frame comes loose and can be tossed down into the skip in the street.

Straighten up to find Alicia, hands on hips, purposefully surveying the newly created hole in the wall. Darryl isn't though. He's watching Alicia. His gaze and stance deliver an unmistakable, testosterone-fuelled, warning of personal possession. Tinged with barely concealed resentment.

I'm not into those games. Stoop and carry on pulling off bits of trailing plaster. Alicia passes over a hammer and a thick stone chisel. "You okay with these? Tidy up the ragged bits. The guide is the line in heavy black marker pen."

"Yeah." Go to work with a will. I like smashing away at inanimate objects. Great stress buster.

Lunch break. Cheese sandwiches prepared by Alicia.

"Fancy a beer?"

"Please."

"Darryl, can you get them?"

He's slow. Reluctant on the ladder. Wait for him to go inside. "Be careful with him."

"What do you mean? He's just an ex-boyfriend helping me out. Sort of..."

"Don't think that's quite how he sees it."

She weighs my comment and dismisses it. "Rubbish. He hasn't a prayer of getting back with me and he knows it. Too immature for a start."

"Okay. Don't say I didn't warn you."

"Warn you about what?" Darryl's head appears over the bay roof edge and then his hand, plonking down three cans of beer, cold from the fridge. Followed athletically by the rest of his lean frame.

"The risk of splinters and not getting them out quickly." Swift improvisation on my part.

"Oh. Have you got something in your hand?" He's not talking to me. Takes her fingers in his rough grip and peers at them.

"It's nothing at all." The irritable note in her voice is very apparent as she shrugs him off. "We need to get on."

Last steps to tidy the edges. Then ropes on the new casement in the front garden and Alicia steadies it from below as Darryl and I haul it up. Much easier with three of us to position and wedge it in place. Supporting screws into the frame along each inner edge. Then filling and making good. Job done. Solid. Needs painting of course. But no good starting that tonight. Going home. Thanks ringing in my ears. From her. Not so much as an acknowledgement from him. Distinct lack of enthusiasm. Even for the fact of my departure.

Get straight at home. Take off my dusty clothes in the kitchen. Stuff them in the washing machine. Wander upstairs naked. One of the privileges of living alone. Shower. Clean jeans. Think about food. Can't be bothered. Open a can of soup. Settle down with the football on the television. Not my team so I'm not particularly into it when the doorbell chimes. Not expecting anyone. Nobody much knows I've moved in. Probably somebody hawking something I've no intention of buying.

But it isn't. This one could sell me anything she wanted. Alicia. A very different woman to the one I was with earlier. This variant is clean, neatly made up, wearing a dress and carrying a bottle of Merlot. "This is me coming to say thank you for helping today."

"You already thanked me. Better come in. It's a bit of a tip though. In fact I'll do you a deal. I'll labourer for you if you help me do my place up."

"Do I look the manual labouring type?"

"Not tonight you don't."

"Good." We've moved into the lounge. She puts the bottle down on the side table. I turn the television off. Mental flash of my mum saying it's rude to keep it on in company.

"Are you going to show me around?"

"If you want to see the house, I will."

Viewing isn't what takes the time. It's exploring the options for change. The potential kitchen extension. The colour scheme and flooring choices for lounge, hall, stairs and landing. The plans for revamping the spare rooms and bathroom. The viability of a loft extension. And how to make the most of the main bedroom which at the moment contains nothing but a king-size bed and a dress rail for my office suits, shirts and ties.

"There's plenty of room for proper built-in wardrobes. And glass sliding doors would save space." She's right on that score.

"Yes. I thought that. And I'll need a chest of drawers. Don't have much furniture yet. My ex-wife kept it all..." Realise Alicia isn't listening. She's sitting on the edge of the bed. Wriggling around. Don't know how else you could describe what she's doing.

"This is very comfortable."

"It was...expensive. A friend told me a long time ago never to stint on your mattress. To get the best you can afford. But I'm not sure you should be sprawled across your boss's bed."

"Money well spent I'd say. And I wasn't sprawling..." Saying which she just lets her body flop backwards. Completely relaxed. "But now I am."

Take the single step forward to put my legs in contact with hers.

"You don't realise just how dangerous a position you're in."

I get a calculating glance up and then away. She's no longer looking at me when she quietly says "Am I worried?"

I was intending to take her hands and pull her to her feet, but common-sense flies clean out the window. I manage to fall beside her rather than across her but that's the last considerate thought I can claim to my credit.

One thing about her dress. It makes things much easier.

"You have got a condom, haven't you?"

"Oh. God. No I haven't."

"Just don't come in me."

The stupid chances we take without conscious thought.

***

"You could stay, Alicia. I mean it's Sunday tomorrow."

"Have to be up early. Lots more to do on the house. But you could come over and help me."

"Will Darryl be there?"

"What difference does that make?"

"You're not that naive. If I'm there it's going to be obvious something's happened between us. We'll be touching each other..."

"Then I won't let you."

"How will you stop me?"

"Good point. And yes, he'll be around. I better find a way of gently easing him out of the picture. I do pay him for his work. Anyway you could come over in the evening if you want to."

"I do want to. Very much. Shall I bring some food so you don't have to cook?"

"Works for me."

"Do I get a last kiss before you go?"

She pauses, kneeling up with one arm into her dress, preparing to pull it on over her head. Shrugs it off. "If you insist."

Which takes another hour.

When Alicia's gone, my stomach realises it needs sustenance after all that exercise. Pull on a shirt and jeans and head out myself. Pick up a Sunday paper and stroll down to a greasy spoon I've discovered which does a great full English breakfast. Run, inappropriately enough, by two German brothers.

An hour idled pleasantly away. Until I get up to pay my bill. Unless I really am losing my marbles, I went to the cashpoint yesterday. There should be fifty quid in my wallet. I'm sure of it. I think. Have to apologise profusely and agree to settle up later.

***

Both Alicia and me yawning all morning. Which would be a dead giveaway if we worked in the same office. Fortunately we reside in separate wings of City Hall and there's not much likelihood of anybody noticing our common condition.

The day does, however, bring yet another difficult conversation with Marianne though to mess up my euphoric mood. Not so much negotiation as confrontation by phone.

"I'm not asking for maintenance."

"I wasn't going to offer any."

"No. Well a clean break then."

"Absolutely."

"Will you leave me the house?"

"You can buy me out if you want to keep it. But why don't you make a new start? In a place that's free of memories of us?"

"I want more than fifty percent. I deserve it."

Have to bite my tongue. Hard. "Even fifty percent of the equity should give you more than a hundred grand. If we sell now."

"I'm not ready to make that decision."

"Okay. But when you are...I think you need certainty though." I really mean that I want finality. "We can do a separation agreement sorting out all the financials even if you want to stay in the house awhile. And divorce can wait a bit." That last comment slips out. I don't mean it at all. The sooner the better. That's what I'm pushing for.

The day passes. And the next few too. Find myself yawning at work more mornings than not. And drowning in novel feelings. So much to marvel over. Like her height. Being on a level when she wears heels. Not having to stoop to kiss her. Like the way she walks, striding out as I do. Not having to pause for her to keep up with me. Like her hair. When the breeze riffles it. It's colour. In fact I love her hair. Her face. It's calmness. The comical, quizzical expressions she pulls. Her legs. As close to perfect as makes no odds. Her feet. All her limbs in fact. But above all else, I love the acuity of her mind. The speed of her analysis of anything and everything and the razor-sharp nature of her responses. There is not an iota of subservience in this woman. She is on every level, an equal, a partner in crime, an instigator of fun. And God help me, for the first time in my adult life, I'm falling without reservations, boundaries or constraints. Something which appears to amuse rather than move her. She seems to have a cool sense of certainty about the feelings she invokes and I can't be sure of anything other than that she relishes being with me. So unless I'm even more of a fool than I take myself to be, I have to trust that, somewhere deep inside herself, she's coming to love me too. Hold my nerve and never, ever question that certainty. If I'm wrong, I'm utterly lost.

Having her sleeping in my bed is mind-blowing. She drives me to make even more effort to ensure her pleasure than my own. I love how her skin responds to my touch, flushing with heat beneath my hands. I'm more aware of the importance of every little clue she yields than any fearful double agent could ever be. I know what makes her shiver with desire. By dint of trial and error, allied to observation, a lovely process, I've discovered most of her sensitivities. I have mapped in my head what will make her tremble and cry out, the pressure points which trigger reactions to be welcomed and what it is which will take her beyond self-control.

The problem is I can see all too clearly that she's learned as much of me. And love and lust are now battlegrounds of matched adversaries on which there is never a clear winner or loser. And that's never been this way for me before. I find I'm waiting to find a catch which keeps on failing to reveal itself. It's just too good. And you know what they say about things that are too good to be true. They usually are.

***

The one obvious fly in the ointment is Darryl. Whatever she means to him, he seems hell-bent on making his existence felt. The week after Alicia started seeing me, I find him loitering outside City Hall as I come out through the main doors. Don't spot him at first. Across the car park. Then his glowering presence registers, but as soon as he twigs that I've spotted him, he turns and saunters away.

"Hey you!"

The only effect is an increase in the speed of his movement in the opposite direction to my route homeward. Consider chasing after him. But that'd be an insult to my dignity. So let him go. Wondering just how much of a problem he's going to make himself.

Forget about him the minute I get in to discover Alicia making Thai prawn curry in my kitchen and one of her favourite trance bands playing on the hifi. She hands me a bottle of cold beer as I walk in. Hard to retain negative emotions in the face of such largesse.

It's Saturday morning when Darryl next makes his presence felt. Pull the curtains back to catch a glimpse of a familiar figure lurking on the opposite pavement. Spotting me at the window, he once again makes off. Consider telling Alicia, but don't. Not sure why not.

***

Take Alicia south west. To meet my mum in Exeter. An early start, a long drive with a short coffee stop at Sedgemoor and a rendezvous beside a parking meter. No time for more than hurried introductions. We've a church service to get to.

The cathedral is laid out for a multi-denominational act of Easter worship. Meaning a marked lack of Anglican formality, a five-piece band at the front, comfortable padded seats for general use by the first-comers, rather than reserved for the great and good of the city, plain printed orders of service bookmarked with long strands of red wool, a lack of hats among the congregation and a surfeit of preachers, several of them wearing sweatshirts emblazoned on the back with the words *Street Pastor.*

The band strikes up. A muted rhythm section. A wash of keyboards. A soaring violin. And a lovely vocalist. Very atmospheric. Not overly religious but who cares?

The thing proper gets underway. It may be ecumenical in intent but it follows a remarkably orthodox structure. Words of greeting. Hymn. Reading. Address. Hymn. Prayers. Hymn. Actually the hymns are problematic. All very modern and therefore un-sing-able. Except 'When I Survey The Wondrous Cross'. Isaac Walton 1674 to 1748. According to the printed Order of Service. Well-seasoned if not downright mature. I much prefer the old ones like this which can be sung with gusto. The ones practised as a youngster in a church choir. In the carefree days post-initiation. Which meant being chased three times round the graveyard and when caught being flung up into the holly bush.

My mobile phone pings during prayers. A text or email. Thought I'd turned the volume off on all functions. Obviously not. Alicia nudges me with her knee. Catch her eye, Find her grinning and raising an eyebrow at me.

We do get to use the red wool, tying knots in it for our loved ones, linking strands with our neighbours and passing them forward to be draped over a cross sculpted from pieces of well-weathered driftwood. An interestingly novel notion.

The inside elements of the service over, we shuffle out slowly amid the crush down the aisle. Sunshine, pouring in, illuminates the nine stained glass panels. Always assumed they were saints but never really looked at them properly before. Surprisingly they're not what I thought they were at all. Except St Peter. Flanking him are figures who must have had long-forgotten links with the city: King Athelstan, Leofric. Stapledon, Edward the Confessor, Queen Edythe, Grandison, Coverdale and Frederick Temple. What on earth did that that lot do to get put up there? Resolve, if I can be arsed, to look them up on-line.

Out into the brilliance of a wonderful spring day. Past Richard Hooker. Don't know who he is either but he's got a rather smart statue, seated on a plinth, surveying all around him. We should be following the crowds behind either the white or purple banners on the so-called Walk of Witness. To watch a mock crucifixion as the Easter message is played out with a cast of amateur actors and a well-behaved donkey wearing a richly ornamented head collar. Trouble is we all know how that story plays out. And the Good Friday bit is both bloody and miserable. Instead the cafe outside the Royal Clarence Hotel calls to us with far greater insistence. To my unexpressed relief it's mum who cracks first. "Let's go and have a cup of tea. I'm not really up to trekking today."

"Alicia?"

"Fine idea."

"Good. The teas are on me then."

"I think I'll have a coffee." Mum changing her mind.

"Two coffees it is. Alicia?"

"Mine's a coke."

The waitress, a Chinese girl all in black, is close enough to hear and correct her. "Pepsi. We have Pepsi"

"That's okay. Doesn't make any difference."

"Some people think it does."

"We're Philistines then." Sticking with biblical themes. "Two cappuccinos and a coke, please."

Drawing the inevitable pedantry of correction. "Pepsi."

"Indeed. That'll do just as well."

A group of young men thread their way past the outlying tables and chairs. Dressed uniformly in red and black track suits. A team then. Not large enough blokes to be rugger buggers. Maybe a soccer side. Come to play Exeter City over the weekend I surmise without any real evidence for that conclusion. Nobody seems much interested.

Mum asks a few questions about Alicia's background and where she comes from. Things I've glossed over a bit myself till now and could stand to know. The answers are fairly uninformative. If not downright evasive. Not for the first time I find myself wondering just what she could be hiding from me.

As soon as she decently can, Alicia changes the subject, pulling yesterday's newspaper from the capacious depths of her shoulder bag. "Have you seen the story about Oxford's Passion Play?"

"No."

"They were refused an entertainment licence by the council. Listen to this. It quotes an Oxford City Councillor; *Unfortunately, one of our licensing officers didn't recognise that a Passion Play on Good Friday was a religious event. I think he thought it was a sex show...* This man obviously needs media training! Even if it's what happened he should know better than to say it to the press."

"Don't believe it."

"It's true. It's here in black and white."

"In the Daily Express."

"Yeah. And your point is?"

"You know what I'm saying."

Before we can develop an argument about journalism in its various forms, Mum steps in. "Did they sort it out in the end?"

"No. It had to be called off. It was all at the last minute."

"Strange things do happen. Do you know the first showing of 'Noah' at our main cinema was cancelled due to overnight flooding?"

"You're kidding."

"Not at all. I cut out the piece about it." My mum's scrapbooks are infamous for reflecting the huge breadth of things which catch her interest. She should have been a librarian or an archivist. Like my Dad. "Can I take that piece about the Passion Play, Alicia?"

"Sure you can."

Coffee arrives along with Alicia's coke. Or rather the substitute offered for the real thing. Not quite sure why but Mum suddenly leans across and says softly to me, "I like her." Nowhere near quietly enough. Alicia tries to suppress a smile.

I don't bother to whisper. "That's good. Think you'll be seeing a lot more of her."

The next beneficiary of our good mood is the Big Issue seller on the corner of Cathedral Yard. He gets a fiver from us and the instruction to "Keep the change."

Alicia stoops to pet his dog. "Half American Pit Bull and half Boxer" he tells us. "She's only two but very sweet natured. And her eyes are both different." They are too. One brown and the other colour-deficient, pale with an albino hint of pink.

"She's great."

"Happy Easter."

"You too."

Take Alicia's hand. No protests. Mum's on the same wavelength and takes her other arm. Frogmarching her off to lunch.

***

The near miss happens after we've eaten and Mum's gone on ahead to get tea ready for us at her flat. Like we need to eat again so soon.

Starting to cross Southernhey. A red car, going too fast, swings round the corner and I have to haul Alicia bodily back onto the pavement. Not so close a call. Just an everyday occurrence, but Alicia's reaction is wholly over the top.

She stands there, in shock, her hands over her face, making little moans of pain.

"Hey...it's alright. Nothing happened." I've got my arms round her but she can't seem to stop shaking. Can hardly stand up. Takes me an age to calm her down. Which is...strange.

***

You'd think that I'd know better than to leap out of the frying pan straight into the fire. But what I do know is that it's not women or even marriage that causes an allergic reaction. It's just being with one particular person. The wrong woman.

And Alicia? For all her foibles, Alicia's different. She makes me smile. And I fancy her like crazy. And even my Mum approves. That's got to be promising. And it was never like this with Marianne. I'm sure of that whatever other doubts I might entertain. So I do what I do. And mostly it's wonderful. Except for not knowing a thing about her background and the problem she only too apparently has with holding onto money. And her ex-boyfriend, the stalker.

***

Darryl's outside my house again exactly a fortnight after his last appearance. Resolve next time I spot him to nip round the back and catch him before he can run away. A few things worth saying to him. It doesn't work out that way. He's not there the following Saturday. Breathe a sigh of relief.

Unfortunately, it doesn't last. On Sunday morning I head out to get the newspapers and my first step out of my front door places my foot on something which bursts open disgustingly and I'm standing on a torn paper bag with my shoe covered in the excrement of some animal with a loose bowel problem. The shoes are fit only for the bin and it takes a pressure hose borrowed from the neighbours to clean off the doorstep.

"What are you doing?" Alicia catching me in mid-clean. No choice now but to tell her. She doesn't want to believe it. "He wouldn't do that."

"I think he just did."

"No. He's harmless."

"Hope you're right." Famous last words.

***

A belated house-warming takes place late in April. An evening far milder than the date gives us any right to expect and since there are only a handful of invitees, we can prepare for both garden and indoor eventualities. The rear half of my new house comprises the kitchen and a dining annexe where the food is laid out. The back door leads into a small garden, terraced and sheltered by old walls reaching head-height. Add a fire-pit purchased from the nearest DIY superstore, rugs, cushions and a few low garden chairs and we can lounge outside in comfort with glasses of wine and musical accompaniment. Thanks for the latter lie with Julie, a friend of Alicia's. She's dragged along a new, and younger, boyfriend, his guitar in one hand and a decent bottle of Chablis in the other.

Clare James, in off-duty mode, brings flowers as well as an amused Patrick Butler, wearing a hefty red sweater, which clashes with his hair, and bearing the obligatory plonk. Jane adds her slightly diffident husband to the mix but he warms up quickly when he realises I'm encouraging him to hold forth on the subjects of construction and renovation, matters of some relevance if I'm to turn this house into what it should become. Mark lives and breathes property - knowledge worth tapping - while Alicia and Jane hunker down, head to head, putting the world to rights, a process involving gentle character assassination of the people we have to work alongside. The ensemble is completed by the arrival of Saul from my gym, who regularly spots for me (and of course vice versa) with his wife Jess, another solicitor. How many lawyers does one small city need?

As an evening, it works. The slightly schizophrenic nature of the food, a collaborative effort between Alicia and me which shows clear evidence of insufficiency of mutual consultation, passes without adverse comment. These are polite guests or maybe just drunken ones. Nobody has to drive and the empty bottles are stacking up. Our musician strums when he feels like it, hugging Julie when he isn't playing, and endears himself to me by having at least heard of Luka Bloom and to Alicia by knowing and rendering versions of two of her favourite songs. Actually making a decent fist of them, singing in a clear but idiosyncratic style, all his own. Moving then into long, interlocking chords. Not attacking them. A smooth and relaxed style of playing. Sounds a bit like the trance music Alicia sticks on in the car. Ask her about it. "Lemon Jelly. Never heard their stuff played this way before. Didn't think it could be done. On an acoustic."

Alcohol loosens inhibitions across the board and it's amusing to note Patrick's hand encroaching on areas a uniformed or less-relaxed version of Clare would probably not allow. At least in company. Jane starts clearing crocks and have to tell her to stop and go back out to talk to the others. Mark is by then semi-recumbent, eyes closed and foot tapping along to the music and Alicia's deep in conversation with Jess.

Saul seizes the opportunity he's clearly been waiting for. Touches my arm to get my attention. Issues an innocuous-sounding invitation. "I've been thinking about putting together a team to do the Three Peaks Challenge next year. For charity. You interested?"

No semblance of thought given to my answer. "Yeah. Why not?"

Clearing up late on Sunday morning. I'm vaguely dressed, if barefoot. Alicia rather less clothed. Not much on beneath her apron. Making it hard to concentrate on the job in hand. She's getting some practice in evading wandering hands and trying to side-track me. "What's that on your t-shirt?"

"The number?"

"Yes."

Don't have to look down to quote it. "Four six six six four."

"And it means...? What does it signify?"

"Guess."

"Haven't a clue."

"It was in the news not so very long ago."

Alicia shaking her head. "I really don't know."

"It's a prison number. Nelson Mandela's when he was on Robben Island."

"Oh!" No smart comment.

As good a time as any to raise something serious. "Alicia?"

"What's up?"

"We can't just go on like this. Can we?"

Bats it back with exquisite calm. "Can't we?"

"Not with you working for me. I'm going to have to talk to the leader. See what he wants me to do."

"And if he says stop seeing me? Would you?"

Shake my head. "Of course not. Find another job, I suppose."

"But you've just got here. He'll be fine you know. Lincoln's too small to be hard and fast on probity stuff. Pragmatic exceptions have to be made. And Neil likes you. Jane told me how much he wanted to get you as Chief Exec as soon as he met you at the preliminary interviews. He won't let you go. Not over me. He'll make it alright."

"Hope you're right."

"Have faith, soldier."

"Okay. Moo-wah"

Alicia's look is one of complete incomprehension.

I spell it out. "M.U.A.A."

Doesn't help much. She still looks baffled. "What?"

"You started it. American military slang. Message understood and acknowledged."

"Okay, soldier. I'm going back to bed. Are you coming with me?"

You bet I am.

***

Arrange to see Neil. Jane gets it organised. "Tell him it's personal."

We sit down in his office. Coffee and small-talk. Feel a strong desire for an alcoholic chaser. Not sure where to start. And Neil doesn't help, withholding any clear opening. Deliberate strategy. Just waiting to hear what I've got to raise with him. Eventually have to break into it. "Got something to share with you. Not sure what I should do about it."

"Yes. And...?"

"I've met somebody."

"Met? Is that a euphemism for finding a girlfriend?"

"It is."

"And that's a problem?"

"Yes. She works for me."

"Not the way I hear it. She works for the Director of Economic Development. Not you. Assuming you're referring to Alicia Valency. Don't look so gob-struck. This is a small place and I make it my business to know what's going on in it. I could probably hazard a guess where you went on your first date if it came to it. So why's it an issue?"

"Because I'm the Chief Executive. And there are rules."

"Don't fraternise with the natives you mean?"

"Something like that."

"But you're single."

"Soon to be divorced. Not quite the same thing."

"I repeat you're a free agent. So's she. She doesn't even report directly to you. There is no problem."

"Well, if you don't think there's one..."

"Not at all. Hope it works out for both of you."

"So if I bring her to a council dinner, you won't mind?"

"You'll raise a few eyebrows. But sod 'em I say."

"Thank you. Can I push my luck and buy her a place on the next twinning trip?"

"Okay. I won't even insist she takes annual leave."

"You are a good man."

"Not what my wife says. Is that all you wanted to talk about?"

"Yep."

"Good." Neil climbs to his feet. "Another meeting to go to then. The story of my life."

Mine too.

Although I'm euphoric that I'm not going to have to choose between Alicia and my job.

***

Given that I seem to have volunteered, it seems incumbent on me to find out exactly what the Three Peaks Challenge entails. I already know it involves climbing Snowdon, Ben Nevis and Scafell Pike. I didn't appreciate that we have to do the whole lot in twenty-four hours, including travelling between them. So it's a challenge that means walking or sprinting around twenty-five miles, much of it straight uphill or down again. And we go for it whatever the prevailing weather and visibility. A tough challenge indeed. And one for which I'm nowhere near fit enough. But at least I've got the sense to admit it to myself. Need to get some proper training in. We've got over twelve months for preparation based on Saul's plan to do it in June next year. But I know just how easily I could postpone doing anything. So I'd better start getting down the gym more regularly.

Look out of my office window, noting with satisfaction the distant cranes. All the signs of construction; of successful economic regeneration policy in action. Love to see brick and concrete outcomes from what we do. And scanning the streets below I like something else. The complete absence of one Darryl Weston. Of such things is happiness made. Even if I'm committed to climbing three sodding mountains.

***

Unfortunately the dog-shit trap isn't the last of Darryl at all. I suffer nails hammered into the side wall of a tyre on two occasions and a firecracker through the letterbox. He's outside City Hall sporadically and then overnight my car's keyed all the way down the near side paintwork. A deep gouge down to bare metal. Nobody heard a thing. The whole road asleep at the time.

When I tell Alicia I've had enough and am going to the police, she begs me not to. "Look I'll go and see him and tell him to stop this." At least she's now acknowledging that in all probability it is him. And, whatever she says, it seems to work. I keep my eyes peeled over the next month and his absence is both complete and welcome.

It's me who raises the matter again. More fool me.

"The Darryl problem seems to have gone away anyway." An odd look flickers over Alicia's face. "What...?"

"He's still emailing me."

"Really."

"Yeah. Most days."

Consternation on my part. "That's sick. Have you told him to stop?"

"Of course I have. It doesn't seem to work. I never reply at all now. What he writes is pretty creepy so I just delete them."

"What's he saying?"

"He keeps on about how we were meant for each other. And that it isn't right me being with an old man like you."

"I'm only thirty eight."

"I know. Not so ancient at all really. So I don't even read them anymore."

"And he's still sending them?"

"Not so many as there were."

"This is harassment. It's a criminal offence. I don't think you should delete them. We ought to save them in a folder in case we need them as evidence. We could get Patrick to send him a warning. A solicitor's letter might make him stop."

"Worth a try."

"Write his address down for me and I'll sort it."

Actually now I know where he is I think I'll pay him a call myself later in the week.

***

It doesn't go well. Delivering the personal message to Darryl. His mother answers the door. A blowsy, red-faced woman. Looking older than her probable age. Alicia neglected to tell me that he still lives at home with his parents. I'm not invited over the threshold and when her son comes down in response to her loud calling, she loiters in the hallway listening to every word. I deliver my warning with great care over my choice of words. Not careful enough though. Before I've even finished she butts in over his shoulder. "You can't talk to him like that."

"Better me than the police. Do you want them involved?"

He looks at me in stony-faced silence. It's his mother who delivers their joint verdict. "Fuck off out of here." No use talking to them. Leave. As instructed.

Walking away down the road helps Darryl find his courage and a voice. He shouts at my back. "You don't know half what's going on. You ain't got a clue. Have you?"

He manages all that without a single swear word.

Keep walking.

***

Neil Wetton was right about one thing. The strength and speed of City Hall's rumour mill. The internal grapevine positively sings with Mayoral Ball gossip. Alicia's presence on my arm can hardly fail to fuel that. For starters she cuts an impressive presence. Making an entrance in a sparkly dress and matching shawl, dotted with tiny stars, around her shoulders. Grey court shoes with heels raising her height close to the six foot mark. All new. And a delicate clutch bag faced with satin roses, a gift from me once I'd seen her intended outfit.

Pause in the doorway to whisper into her artfully exposed ear. "I've got a problem with your dress." Flick her star-shaped earring with my forefinger. It swings to and fro brushing against her earlobe.

"Now you tell me. What's wrong with it?"

"Nothing. But how am I expected to keep my hands off you all night?"

"Behave, soldier." Mock glower. Hope it's a pretence anyway. "Come on, we're up."

And we follow the mayor and sheriff and their ladies into a hall of guests on their feet, applauding enthusiastically. Which when you've done nothing to deserve it, feels pretty odd let me tell you. It can also, like the unstintingly served wine, go to your head, if you let it. I try not to.

Not so sure about Alicia. The flush of pleasure across her face lasts all evening. And it doesn't come from the sip or two she takes from her wine-glass or the small taster of port towards the end of the dinner. And it's unlikely to be the solitary cup of tea, which necessitates the trips, too many eyes on her, to find the toilet. She seems to stand even more regally upright as she moves across the floor, revelling in the attention and the only partially masked observations and the scandalous insinuations muttered as she passes.

When she comes back, she seems to stand a fraction longer beside me than strictly necessary, looking about her, with a hand on my dinner-jacketed shoulder, surveying the room. Smiling. In the public gaze. And magnificent as she looks, I can't help asking myself if her enjoyment is entirely healthy and innocent. And I'm not sure why that thought should even occur to me. Nor why I should so carelessly feed it as we leave the hall at the end of the night, as she insouciantly accepts as her right the appreciative tap my flattened palm places on her wonderfully tempting arse.

***

According to Alicia the emails falter and dry up when the solicitor's letter goes out. But that happy state of affairs lasts all of five days. "He's started up again. Three today."

"You mean Darryl?"

"Who else?"

"Not much choice then. I'm going to raise it with Clare."

"I'd rather you didn't. He will stop eventually."

"You think so."

"Yes."

"I'm glad you do. I just don't believe he will. How many months has it been now? Too many!"

"Please. Leave it for now. I'm keeping them all as evidence. Like you said. So we can bring the police in when we need to. If it gets worse. For now let it lie. I'm going to speak to him."

Against my better judgement, I listen to her and do nothing.

***

The Mayor's Ball is a marker of sorts. The end of the fun and games which must now give way to the serious business of creating a new administration.

First Thursday in the merry month of May. Election Day. One third of the seats on the council up for grabs. One in each of the eleven wards. Always an interesting time. This is a city which swings slowly between polar extremes. At one time it was one hundred percent Labour, with no opposition other than a self-created one inside the party group. It's a very different situation now and who knows what its final political composition will look like when we've finished counting the contents of all the ballot boxes in the early hours of tomorrow morning.

An old proverb says *Learn another language, gain a second soul.* Well the public sector certainly has its own vernacular but I don't think understanding its complexities gives me anything beyond some unusual skills which earn me a living. A special subset of that jargon and those skills comes into play for only this one day every year. Or to be exact three years out of four for the council, every third year for the county council and every five years for a general election and at God-knows what interval for anything connected with the European Union.

It's always a strange day: Election Day. Exciting in its own way and a real break from routine enjoyed by all the staff caught up in it. I suspect it's equally thoroughly dreaded by those standing for office. Get into the office just after seven o'clock by which time the polling stations are all open. Work out which I want to visit to get a sense of what's happening and to check for potential problems. Coffee with my deputies and delegate the rest of the visits to them. The ones I don't want to do myself.

Get on the road. A circuit taking in each of the church halls and schools I've chosen and I really want to see the fish and chip shop we use on an estate where there's nowhere else to issue ballot papers to voters. Pass a chunk of the morning talking to Presiding Officers and Poll Clerks and chatting with counting agents and candidates wherever they turn up. The one place I don't go is the hall where Alicia will be in charge until polling finishes at nine sharp. I want to very much but manage to keep myself from going anywhere near her.

Back in the office find Neil sweating on the suspected swings identified on the ground by his volunteers. He knows better than to haunt neutral territory which today is my office, the Returning Officer's base, so I run into him in the corridor heading for the members library. He's done pretty much everything he can out on the stump, electioneering, canvassing and encouraging turn-out. To stay calm now and let what happens just happen is a big ask for a political animal used to being in control. And his future hangs in the balance if his majority is reduced. He looks really harassed.

"How's it going?"

And I get back a shake of the head and two words "Who knows?" And he's right. At this stage nobody does.

Stroll around town and bring back sandwiches. For Jane and me.

The afternoon's quieter. A sign that good order prevails out there. No problems. So my people tell me as they report in. And City Hall itself is like a morgue. Core services only and few visitors. Most of the staff busy on election duties. No meetings in the diary. Do a bit of work on some files and walk home to get myself tea. Half expecting my mobile to ring. Alicia or trouble or both. It doesn't.

Back into town to the Drill Hall set up for tonight's count. Find nothing much to do there either except read the newspaper. It only gets busy much later when the counting staff, most of them recruited from local banks and building societies, trickle in.

The tables are finally full and all the stationary and supplies distributed just before close of poll. And delivery of the ballot boxes starts. Alicia arrives with a clerk some fifteen minutes later so she's among the first. She grins across at me and gives me the thumbs up before dumping her boxes and heading out again. So she's enjoyed her day.

Then it gets frantic for an hour or so until all the ballot box contents have been verified against each Presiding Officers' accounts and the formal business of counting votes is underway; a second measured and careful stage moving towards the main highlights, announcing the results for each ward. Along the way a few personal favourite moments when I get to explain to the candidates which ballot papers I'm disqualifying. There are the ones who voted for too many candidates or put their own name on the paper or left it blank. I can't help but enjoy their faces when I tell them "This voter thinks you're all Nazis. This one says *None worth a vote*. This one has the word *shitheads* on it." Usually a choice few like that. Protest votes if you like.

Results out about half two in the morning. Neil's still in charge with a yet more slender overall majority in the council. So to clearing up whatever won't wait for the day shift. One of my people offers me a lift home but I want to walk. It's only a mile or so and it's a lovely night to put one foot in front of the other, clearing away all the stuffiness and relishing the quiet satisfaction of a well-administered process.

The key turns in the lock. The lights downstairs are still on. And the television. Walk in to find Alicia watching the regional results for the East Midlands.

"Hi you."

"Hi you too. Want to watch this?"

"No. Think I'll have a cup of tea."

She gets up. Gives me a hug. "I'll make it. You go to bed. I'll bring it up to you."

Do as she says, shedding clothes on the rug. Asleep as soon as my head hits the pillow. The tea never gets drunk.

CHAPTER IV: MAY TO JUNE

Pre-meeting with Clare on the crime and disorder agenda for the city. Doesn't take too long. Lots of accord and goodwill between council and police. Clare, standing to leave, spots the pile of holiday brochures on my desk. "Going somewhere?"

"City break. Want somewhere lovely and fun." Not telling her I want to be somewhere with Alicia where we definitely won't be bumping into Darryl.

"Something romantic?" A calculating expression accompanying the two word interrogation. Plenty of sub-text.

Deadpan nod. "Yes." I can admit that much.

"Any front-runners?"

"Been considering Prague."

"My brother swears by Istanbul. If you want exotic."

"That's a thought."

It is too. Quite a thought. Head over to Waterstones for a guidebook. Skim-read chunks of it. And the decision's made. Go home to persuade Alicia. Assuming persuasion's necessary. Turns out it's not.

***

I like to plan. Hence reading the guidebooks. In the plural. Discussing what I've learned with Alicia is the order of the day. Rules for Turkey. Not for the beach. That's a whole different and easier issue. Even though it's purportedly an open society, in the cities you dress fairly modestly, especially if you're a woman. Not in shorts or mini-skirts or skin-tight jeans. And you don't wear military gear. This is a country subject to military rule in living memory, so khaki and camouflage is for the army and they like to keep it that way. And secular it may still be, but its Muslim face is more apparent these days. More women in burkas or hijabs on the street than you'd have seen twenty years ago. The secularism of Ataturk is being eroded and female deputies are now being permitted, if not actively encouraged, to wear headscarves to cover their hair in parliament, something expressly prohibited by the constitution for decades. But hopefully the lurch towards religious observance is no more than another hiccup in the long history of tolerance, punctuated by politically advantageous purges, which marks Byzantium, Constantinople and Istanbul's existence.

So book, pack, go.

***

The lads in the airport duty-free gadget shop are indulging in good-natured banter. Two black guys, one white. Not that the dispute's split along ethnic lines. They're arguing about special neck cushions. One of them has hooked his samples over the counter edge and a colleague reckons they're in the way of the till.

"Nobody'll want to buy a pillow anyway, wherever you display them. They can get free use of one on the plane if they want."

Poke my oar in. "No squabbling please. Not over cushions."

The salesman behind the counter laughs. "Haven't you ever heard of pillow-fights?"

"Only as a kid."

One of the others chimes in. "Would you like to buy one then?"

Shake my head. "More concerned about you lot. Working together."

"Ah but we've got the camera on." Gestures up at the mini-CCTV unit on the wall. "The boss'll know he started it."

"I certainly didn't."

"Course you did. You stuck those cushions in my space. Now you going to take them away or what?"

Drift off leaving them to it. Glad they're having fun in the job. Passing their time productively. Wander over to find Alicia at a perfume stand. Dabbing on something from an oddly shaped tester. She cocks her neck for me to sniff. "What do you think?"

"Yeah..." It's strong. And about as practical as the design of its bottle.

"Okay. That's a no then." Picks up a little box containing her favourite fall-back. "You getting this for me then?"

Kick myself. Should have seen that coming and offered first. Take it from her with good grace. Over to the desk to pay for it. Fumble to find my boarding card to show them I'm entitled to buy duty free goods. The price still leaves me unconvinced it's any cheaper than on the high street. But I'm not a regular perfume-buyer so how would I know? Lot of money for a tiny amount of fluid is where I'm at. It's handed over in a pretty, pink promotional bag.

"Thank you, soldier." Get a kiss as well and an arm linked in mine.

"Coffee?"

"Get a newspaper too and we can do the crossword together." Which is what we do. Until we have to scrabble all our gear together and run to the gate for the final call to board.

Last Call. Now there's a misnomer. At the gate, boarding hasn't even started. Even though take-off's supposedly no more than twenty minutes away. So that's not happening on time. "Problem with our new ground handlers." According to the First Officer over the intercom once we're in our seats. "They aren't very good." We lose our runway slot in consequence. Wait on the tarmac for another twenty-five minutes, restless to be under way. Eventually we get to fly, but we don't make up the lost time in the air.

Late landing at Kemal Ataturk Airport. At least the pre-booked taxi's still around, the driver leaning on the rail in arrivals holding a plastic board, our names written on it in chino-graph pencil. Patchy traffic delays us further and we're much later than expected getting up into Sirkeci. Then the driver seems to have no clue where our hotel is. We go round a few of the narrow streets twice before he decides to park up, take our cases out and indicate for us to follow him on foot, in and out of a rabbit warren of old buildings. Until somebody helpfully points him in the right direction and with a sigh of relief he dives into the right one, ensuring we're close on his tail. Takes us inside the lobby, apologising profusely. In Turkish so we don't understand a word. Accepts a tip he doesn't deserve with a polite little bow and leaves us to the tender mercies of the night staff.

Travel weary and close to collapse. Cups of tea. The room and the large divan with the folded down crimson bedspread look incredibly inviting. Use them. Crash out.

***

The morning vista from our room isn't promising. From our second floor window the view is of a grey backstreet - flats dotted with washing lines and dust-beaten carpets. But we've slept soundly. The bed's comfortable and the shower's hot. So far so good.

Umit, or the man behind the desk wearing the badge carrying that name, indicates the lift. Says "Breakfast on top floor." Economy of words. But what a revelation they cover because the roof garden is something else. Stunning.

Alicia's "Wow!" is all she can get out. And that's more than I can manage until I've taken in the view and shaken my head in wonder. In bright sunlight we're looking across at Hagia Sophia, the earliest and greatest cathedral in Christendom, at the Blue Mosque across the square, at the Bosphorus and at the Sea of Marmara, the waters calm beneath blue skies. The worst cup of coffee in the world would taste sublime from this vantage point. But in fact the coffee's pretty good. And below us, in the foreground, beside the tram lines, we overlook a smaller place of worship at the roadside and the soundtrack rising in the clear air is the hubbub of conversation interrupted every few moments by the spasmodic clang of a tram's warning bell.

No rush over breakfast. The buffet is well stocked with fruit, yogurt, salads, cold meats and cheeses and chafing dishes hold sausage slices in spicy tomato sauce and boiled eggs. Can't find it in me even to be particularly annoyed by the loud German tones around us or the nasal Americanisms; the word *Awesome* periodically punctuating conversation like a transatlantic full stop.

We sit over our food in a haze of wordless pleasure. Then go out, hand in hand, to explore the magical new world before us. Pretty rapidly find we don't stand out that much, the tall red-haired surveyor in the long cotton skirt and the pale-skinned lawyer in jeans and sandals. Not amongst the polyglot flotsam which washes around the heart of this vast city. Everywhere we come across people who respond to us because we're English and because we're trying to use the painfully few words of Turkish we've learned in advance. English it seems is the second language of preference for Turks to learn and most of the shopkeepers and restaurateurs claim to have either worked in England themselves at one time or another, or to have family who still do.

For our first day we just want to see everything. Which is, of course, impossible. The obvious place to go first is just across the square opposite the block of buildings containing our hotel. To see Hagia Sophia. A queue, not unexpectedly, for the cathedral but not too long to wait before we can pass in through tall double doors into the cool interior. Into a vast space. Seen from the inside the great dome is an amazing structure, still bearing, after all the years of Moslem domination, the gold-embellished Byzantine images of the Madonna and child, of the city's saints and rulers. Alicia starts to say something. Don't catch it. Ask her what. She says "Shush." Walks down to the front of the church, me at her heels. To where a small square of stone slab floor is protected with crimson velvet rope. A little sign tells us why. In Turkish, English and German. Here, under the watchful gaze of the Holy Virgin, Byzantine emperors were crowned.

Find the stairs up to the galleries. Not so much stairs as a cobble-stoned ramp inside a tower. Taking us up to where courtiers and empresses watched services below and chattered in low and not so low tones. Long, long ago. Lean on the rail. Seeing what they saw. And feeling a very powerful sense of peace. Not thinking to break it, I pull Alicia closer and kiss her softly. For drawn-out moments neither of us wants to move out of this embrace. So we don't.

Back in the street at last, we're almost over-awed by what we've seen. No way am I going anywhere else, let alone shopping in the bazaar, Alicia's next choice, until we've had the chance to sit down, grab a drink and absorb where we've just been. Just as well Alicia feels the same way. We find another high roof garden over a good hotel and take cappuccinos there looking across the oldest quarter of the city. Have it to ourselves apart from the smiling bartender. He's doubtless seen his fair share of lovers among his customers and knows full well how to remain discreetly in the background until the exact moment we need our cups refilled and then he's there almost before we formulate the notion that another coffee would be nice.

We do move on of course and come close to losing each other in the hurly-burly of the Grand Bazaar. It only takes a brief distraction, one of us stopping to look at a stallholder's wares coupled with momentary inattention by the other, walking on into the crowd. Eventually we resort to holding hands. As precautionary measures go, hardly distasteful. And we do stop to buy. Boxes of chewy, nutty, fruit treats. A set of glass tea cups with dinky little spoons. A tee-shirt for Alicia: decline to get one myself and become her clone. Scarves; rich, golden yellow for her, turquoise and brown for me. Full marks for trying for the vendor who, guessing our nationality, shouts across loudly "I can help you spend your money here, my friend." Demanding a response in kind.

"I'm sure you could. Not today though!"

More cappuchinos sitting at a table at the intersection of four lanes of stalls. The ideal spot for people-watching. The clash of cultures epitomised by the laughing girl in the blue jeans and platform shoes, her head swathed in a hijab. Looking mysterious and wonderfully sexy at one and the same time.

We manage an hour. Weariness is setting in. Come across a tea garden which looks a good place to sit. Quaffing black tea, or in Alicia's case, the peppermint variety, served with a side order in the shape of a slice of gelatinous Turkish Delight studded with pecans and almond flakes. On the table in front of us I put my little Anglo-Turkish dictionary and the notebook in which I'm diligently transcribing new words and phrases to learn. The toilet please; *tuvalet lutfen*. I'd like a red wine; *Istiyorum bir sarap kirmizi*. And *Zeytin*. We both love olives so that seems a good word to learn. What else should I be putting down for future use?

"Excuse."

Look up and a dark little man with a neat goatee is standing beside us. Head inclined politely. Holding a file in his hands. "I see you try to learn our language. I learn English. Is my day off. Can I get more tea? I can sit with you and talk if you like."

"Your English is very good. Much better than our Turkish."

"Ah. But I learn a long time."

Flash a glance at Alicia. She nods her agreement and smiles. "Of course. Please sit with us."

"Let me order." He snaps his fingers and another of the myriad idling waiters leaps to do his bidding.

Befriending Amal turns out to be a sound move. Instead of continuing an afternoon's tiring sight-seeing, we get some insight into Turkish mores and customs. Amal is unusual. Not only well educated; he works at the university; but he's also from a religious minority. He's a Christian in this secular state which gives him an unusually broad mindset. And he's saving to get married. In another five years he thinks he'll have enough money put by to meet the material demands of his in-laws-to-be who want a three-piece suite, a fridge, a freezer, a new television and a washing machine as a dowry for allowing him to marry their daughter. Who he loves inordinately and is prepared to wait for even though her family is being over-greedy and he's already thirty-two years old. This all takes two refills of our glass tea-cups to discover and we're making a start on a couple of key phrases we ought to learn when there's another greeting. This time very obviously not a local man, however heavily bearded.

"*Merhaba*, Amal. Who are your friends?" A tall man with a large paunch. His accent strong and its origin obvious.

"Hello. This is Michael. He comes here of Belfast."

"From Belfast" comes the correction. "We say from a place, not of a place."

"Thank you."

"Would you like to sit down." Alicia taking the initiative. Gives Michael our names. "We're English as you can doubtless tell. We're from Lincoln."

"I will join you. And I may be from Belfast but now I live here. And I'm almost Turkish."

"Could have fooled me."

"You didn't hear me before I emigrated."

"What do you do here?"

"I write. And I'm a photographer. And I publish art books. Including my own. But mostly I live on my pension." He holds up his left hand. Three of the fingers are missing above the first joint. "Factory accident. Many years ago when I was a student. Working in the holidays. I invested my compensation wisely. And here I am."

Amal interrupts. "He is a very rude man, Michael. He plays games with his hand."

"I'm not sure you should put it like that, Amal." Michael's laughter is a bull-like bellow. "He means I have some party tricks for strangers. Takes a packet of Polo Mints out of his trouser pocket. Doesn't offer them round. Extracts two, puts them on his tongue and manoeuvres them into a bulging cheek. "Now watch. Imagine you didn't know about my fingers and all you saw was this." He crams the tips of his ruined fingers unnaturally deeply into his mouth and bites into the mints with a crunching sound and carries on chewing. Loudly. The effect is very disquieting. He retrieves his hand and swallows the sweets. "Or there's this one. Makes a fist with just the stump of his index finger sticking out. Puts it up one nostril and wiggles it about. If he had a normal length of finger it'd now be prodding around inside his brain.

Which is exactly how it would appear to an unsuspecting eye-witness. Again the huge laugh as Michael sees our stunned faces.

"That's a trick and a half."

"Got to make some positive mileage out of my infirmity. As well as the money."

More tea. More conversation. More Turkish words. Amal writes them neatly down for me in my notebook. I write a few English phrases he's unsure of into his file. In the end we all part, exchanging addresses, as firm friends.

"If you and your lady come here again - you write to tell me. And I take you to dinner. Show you around. Is that how you say?"

"Very good. And thank you. *Tesekkurederim*." We've got that one nailed now.

***

After dinner we carry on strolling. Find a large bar promising live entertainment. Unspecified. The posters outside show traditional Turkish misicians, a snake-charmer with a huge python slung around his shoulders and whirling dervishes. So the little suitcase wheeled in and left untouched on the club's stage under the central spotlight for several minutes isn't exactly what we expect.

A drum-roll grabs our attention and the thing starts to unzip itself. A large male hand emerges first and then, sinuously smoothly, an entire body emerges, naked except for a spangled leotard, unwraps itself and assumes an upright position, standing free of the case but with one foot tucked firmly behind one ear and hands outstretched to implore the applause he gets in spades.

I can't begin to describe all the positions the contortionist is able to adopt. Many of them don't look even remotely anatomically feasible. As though he's made of rubber and every hinged element of his body is double-jointed. At the end he wields a tennis racket in the spotlight. De-stringed. He pulls some girl tourist up onto the low stage to test its frame is solid before insinuating his whole body through it. One arm first. Then his head and neck. The other arm bending improbably back on his shoulder blade, he brings the racket down. Wriggles it across an undulating chest and stomach, his belly sucked in. Hollowed like a starving man's cheeks. Wrenches his hips and buttocks through the frame so he can step cleanly out of it and vanishes in a puff of sweetly scented smoke. As purple strobe flashes dazzle his audience. Astonishing. A roaring acclaim. Everybody on their feet clapping. But he doesn't reappear.

The background music restarts and people reluctantly dive back into their drinks and conversations.

"How about that, A?"

"Can't quite believe what I've just seen, soldier. Wonder what he gets up to in bed." A dirty, gurgling laugh.

"Trust you. Want another glass of wine?"

"Not really. Unless you want one. Let's go."

We head out. Arms around each other. No need to talk. Comfortably attuned to each other's silence. Stopping occasionally to look at the passing ships plying their trade up and down the Bosphorus. Kissing gently. An entirely satisfactory way to amble back in the general direction of the old town and our hotel. The dome and minarets on the skyline catch the moonlight as I kiss Alicia again for good measure. Everything about tonight demands passion.

Recrossing the Galata Bridge. Into another bar. A place underneath the bridge where there's live music, a trio playing a soulfully modernised form of regional music, a wailing Arabic sound set against a steady beat. And in an almost empty room, a laughing Turkish family at the next table to the one we take. I'd guess they're a father and mother with their son and daughter-in-law. Enjoying a few glasses of wine and a plate of bread and olives.

The musicians don't seem to care that they have little by way of an audience. They're giving it their all. In a world of their own. And the older man at the next table stands up, extending his hand in a timelessly formal gesture to his wife. Despite her girth, she rises gracefully to take it and moves with him onto the little strip of clear wooden floor in front of the band. Steps into his arms and dances as though, at this very moment in time, nobody else matters in their world. And I'm suddenly so envious of their ease with themselves and the depth of their obvious affection for and pride in each other, I have to look away. It's simply too intimate.

The woman returns to their table first, trailing her man behind her. She doesn't pay us the slightest attention as she passes us. But he does. Pauses right there in front of us. It's so clear he knows we've been watching them dance. Says something solemnly I don't understand in Turkish. Places a gentle hand on Alicia's head and holds his other hand out for me to shake. A blessing of sorts.

A few minutes later the family are gone. The band's packing up and some record or other is playing. A song I vaguely know - something with both Western and African elements. A lyric about time and a line repeated mentioning passing seconds. I don't feel we should sit here any longer. I fear saying something stupid. Telling Alicia how much I love her. The very thing I know she doesn't want to hear.

Turning into our narrow little street. "Nightcap? Coffee? Brandy?"

Alicia negates the suggestion. "Had enough. Need my bed."

Know we'll sleep soundly. We definitely should.

We don't.

***

Something wakes me up in the middle of the night. Not a sound. More a sense of disturbance in the air. Eyes acclimatise slowly to the pitch darkness. To find Alicia sitting bolt upright in bed. Her fist in her mouth. Muffling any noise she might unintentionally loose. But the tears trickling down her face give her away completely and utterly.

An arm around her shoulder and she starts to shake. Her body crumples and twists. Ends up in my arms. But far from calmly. Sobbing harder against my chest.

"What is it, girl? You can tell me."

"Nothing! Nothing!" There's a useless lie if ever there was one.

"It's not nothing. I'm here. Let it out."

"Can't." And the crying goes on until she's worn herself out. Let her down gently onto the pillow.

She mutters something.

"I didn't catch that. What did you say?"

No response. She's asleep again. Sit in a growing half-light, getting cold. It's nearly morning. I could swear that the last thing she uttered was a question. "Did you think you could save me?"

***

In the morning, try to talk to Alicia about the night terrors and it's as though she either doesn't or can't remember at all or refuses to. And another day starts just like yesterday. Just like each and every day starts. With cheese, meat, olives and bread rolls consumed with that fabulous view before us. But down there we'll find something different to see. And we'll be walking our legs off again. Almost.

It's warm but not too hot, the sun pleasant on our shoulders. The roof garden's nearly full. Have to share a table. The middle-aged couple there before us grunt some form of greeting and hide behind their newsprint. A woman's magazine and De Telegraaf. Dutch then. Don't mean to pry but you can't help glancing across and if you recognise something... It's on the sports page; a headline and the sub-paragraph below it in bold containing the words *Voetballer*, *Ajax* and *Lenahan*. Is that Lincoln City's star striker on the move then? The one with the criminal father? Bought and sold? Good luck to him if that's the case. Someone getting to follow their dreams. Try to draw it to Alicia's attention without appearing too rude to the Dutch couple. Before the page is folded back out of sight. She's oblivious. Have to remember to tell her later. Without fail. Really must.

Out onto the streets for our second day of wandering. Gazing. Tasting the sights. Around the streets near the hotel. Then widening the search zone to take in Gulhane and Eminonu. Stopping for tea or coke. Or better still the tart refreshment of freshly pressed pomegranate juice. Complete with seeds. A single Turkish lira buys a small home-made apple turnover, dusted in icing sugar, which melts in my mouth. And don't get me started on how good the banana, cream-filled, pastries are. Street vendors wander between the outdoor tables from diner to diner, offering flowers, packs of paper handkerchiefs, leather wallets and reading glasses. Or watches, the chosen specialty of African immigrants, circles of them on each dark-skinned arm, perfectly displayed. The tempting smells of cooking meat and fish are constant. God help a vegetarian here! And caffeine addicts can get a fix on any corner. Think Turkish coffee or cappuccinos in the more cosmopolitan bars. Or anything at all in the Starbucks concessions springing up as part of a thankfully limited incursion into Istanbul's culinary traditions and habits.

And you can't not buy stuff. The art of the hectoring traders demands you do. And Alicia and I have the limited resistance of any first-time arrival on the cusp between Europe and Asia. We choose ceramic bowls, tins of apple tea and more scarves in vibrant colours. We even think about a wall-hanging - a piece of Suzani, stylized flowers on a richly coloured velvet backing - the laughing shop-keeper extracts a promise from us to return.

Back for afternoon tea at our hotel, looking out over the city, talking quietly about home, work and emotions. Always found it easy to be open about how I'm feeling when I'm allowed to be. And, up to a point, she reciprocates, but so obviously exercising care about what she says. However she dumps one real surprise on me.

"It's not changed that much."

Look at her askance. Puzzled would be an understatement. "You've been here before?"

66

"A long time ago. Many years." And Alicia drops a new bombshell. "Came with my husband."

"You've been married?" Stupid question. Having once had a spouse rather implies marriage.

"Yes. Didn't I say before?"

"No you bloody didn't." No heat in it. Just a dose of confusion. "When? You're divorced?"

"Yes. It didn't last that long. Two and a bit years. That's all."

"What happened? Who was he? Where is he now? What went wrong?" I could drop a myriad other questions into the pool of our afternoon but those'll do for starters.

"I'm not sure I want to talk about it. It didn't end...very well. That's a three glasses of wine conversation."

"Why three glasses?"

"One to loosen my mouth and two more to loosen my brain so the truth pours out."

"So if I want to know what's really happened in your life, I should dose you with red wine?"

"On an empty stomach. Better than sodium pentothal and a lie-detector."

"Is that a fact? So now I know what we're doing tonight."

"What?"

"Drinking."

"We certainly are not, soldier. I want to go and see the whirling dervishes. The ones on the poster in the lobby."

"Sounds like avoidance to me."

"Call it what you like. I'd rather be entertained than interrogated."

She closes down all avenues for raising questions on the subject of her former husband, the way she does with so many matters she regards as personal and deeply private. The very opposite of me. I can be open to the point of being stupidly transparent. So he, whoever he is and what happened between them, is dropped as a subject. Completely and utterly. And remains un-resurrected, for lack of any offered opening, for the rest of our stay. But the questions? Ah, the questions linger on in the ether.

***

The Istanbul-card is a masterstroke. It gives us the tram to Kabitas and the ferry out to The Princes' Islands for starters. At the loading bay, a crowd surges onto the boat, heading for the open-air seats at the back. It becomes obvious why as the journey gets underway. Here is where it all happens. Inside is merely a sedate place for marking time. Out on the deck arguments and laughter reign. Black tea is served in miniature glass beakers, strong and sweet. Accompanied by a simit, one of the large salty pretzel rings, carried around stacked high, one-handed, on a massive tray. Failure to anticipate the motion of every wave, the slightest stagger, and the whole lot comes down to be kicked into the scuppers. But the vendor never fumbles, never lets a single one drop.

Uneaten bread is tossed overboard in chunks for the swooping gulls. Their quarrelsome chittering, as they keep pace with us, is un-awed by our closeness. Rather they stall and glide almost in our faces.

Kadikoy, the first stop on the Asian side, mills with manoeuvring vessels and impatient people. The boats lined up along the moorings bear exotic names. Yeni Yesil Ada, Hafim Inandi, Yazici IV, Bosfer and Kaptan Mustafa Guler. The noise of the people, the seabirds and the engines reach a raucous pitch. Only the hundreds of cormorants on the seawall sit impassive, above it all. Their gaze is westward, out to sea. When each is ready, it dives purposefully straight down into the cold water, coming up with the deep swallowing motion so typical of long-necked, aerial, predators.

Underway again. Something tickling my ear. Turn to get a face-full of the curly, wind-whipped hair of the woman sitting behind us. Alicia catches my startled expression on film, taking picture after picture with her long-lensed camera. On the port side the southward urban sprawl of this enormous city. To starboard, sparkling open water and then as each island comes into view, Kinaliada, Burgazada and, Heybeliada, clumps of afforestation, rocky beaches and townships which are little more than strings of bars and hotels. A touch of the Florida Keys about them. Hemingway would have felt at home here. Mind you we don't see Sivriada, uninhabited apart from the ghosts of all the stray dogs rounded up in the city and transported there to starve to death in crueller times, over a century ago.

Landfall at Buyukada. Famished. Walk down the front and a restaurant takes our fancy, for no reason beyond the owner's gentle smile of welcome and the amusing cliché of its name. Ali Baba's. We choose mezes. Spicy radishes stuffed with cream cheese. Anchovy-wrapped olives, taramasalata and chopped peppers. Washed down with crisp white wine. Fuel for the walk inland. Ignore the importuning of the phaeton drivers. I want clean air away from the acrid scents of horse urine and dung which clog the town centre. It's not too hot but the sun slants into our eyes. We haven't brought sunglasses with us. So we buy cheap imitation Ray Bans which change colour, blue and green, in the light.

Leave the tourist stalls and bars behind. They give way to paved streets of tall, wooden houses, some grandly appointed with mature trees and hanging vines, others decaying, their white and cream paint peeling off in onion-skin layers and their boards lifting to reveal the sickening sight beneath of the bloated orange masses formed by dry rot. There was a lot of money here once and signs that some might still remain.

Alicia takes more photographs. "It reminds me of New Orleans or even Havana" she says. "Ever been?"

"Not yet."

"Then I'll take you. One day."

Walking on, arms round each other's waists and contentment in every step.

I haven't actually told Alicia what we're going to see. I'm looking for a little side street off the main drag, running downhill to the shore. When I find and turn into it, she says "You're up to something."

"Maybe."

"What is it?"

"You'll see. Probably not that exciting. Just something I thought we should do."

She kisses my cheek which I presume indicates approval. Modern signalling methods in action.

We stop outside a stone cottage, last white-washed a half century or more ago, standing in an overgrown little garden, the trees touching its walls and hemming it in as much or more than the padlocked gate and the rusty old bars.

"It's not a patch on the mansions on the road." Alicia stating the obvious with a gleeful glint in her eye.

"No. But then again a very famous man came here to hide away and write the history of his revolution. He didn't choose to live on the mainland but on this little island. He didn't want to live in a house in plain view. He chose to be as far away from others as he could. He probably kept the gates locked except when he took a walk to sit down there by the sea, on his own in splendid isolation. And he was right, wasn't he? Because when they caught up with him in Mexico, they buried an ice-pick in his head."

"They didn't." Alicia's completely wrapped up in the tale. "Who was he?"

"He was a scholarly little man who wore spectacles. And his name was Leon Trotsky. And his crime was to fall out with Stalin."

"Did he have a family? A wife he loved? Children?"

"I don't know. We'll have to read up on him."

She looks up and down the hill. Scans the high boundary walls and the thick undergrowth barring the path down to the sea. And I swear my self-reliant, tough sweetheart sheds a tear for him. Right then and there.

***

It's dark re-crossing the sea of Marmara. A cool wind blowing over the churning water. Alicia nestles in the crook of my arm, my jacket around her shoulders. She's almost asleep, uttering nothing save an occasional sigh as I squeeze her waist or kiss her forehead. Cabin-less fishing boats drift past, tossing in the ferry's wake, their little riding lights, atop tall poles, bobbing hypnotically up and down. Larger craft shadow us; other passenger boats, coasters and tugs, all keeping close in to shore. When she does say something, it feels enormously significant.

"This has been the best day ever."

"Tomorrow will be the best day too" I promise. "And the day after that."

***

It's a promise which struggles to survive the next morning. Heading north-east. On foot. Over the Galata Bridge. Past the fishermen and the little stands of carelessly presented small sea creatures for sale in plastic cups of briny water. Walk along the bay. Past the fenced off moorings of the massive cruise-liners. Ignoring the small enclave of doubtlessly expensive shops and refreshment stalls where the two-hour visitors can make-believe they've actually landed in and seen Istanbul as part of their round-the-world trip.

Arriving at last at a little park where we can buy cups of tea and sit in the shade of a beautifully-rendered modern sculpture of a man holding a small child. Or is the androgynous creature a woman? My feet are sore and make the mistake, against Alicia's best advice of taking my shoes off. That I should have listened to her becomes obvious when I try to put them back on. She laughs at the struggle. Can't blame her. Instead of becoming annoyed, as I doubtless would've with Marianne, I find I'm laughing too and it's a revelation.

Push on with the last short leg of our trek to the Dolmabache Palace to find it closed. "Exceptionelle." The attendant manning the x-ray machine, a key component of Palace security, pronounces it as though speaking French. "Open Tuesday" he pronounces. Too late for us. He lets us through to look into the courtyard but that's it and we're back out on the street.

There's no way we're walking all the way back which is when we take that taxi. It's not as though we're naive or stupid. We ask the skinny, balding man in the grey tweed jacket beside his yellow cab, the fare to Hagia Sophia. "*Kacha?*"

He says "English?" Points inside the car. "I not over-charge. Good Muslim. Lira? Euro? You be happy."

"About how much?"

He shrugs. "Busy road. But I have meter."

Get in and he immediately pushes through three lanes of moving traffic to make the turn we need. Starts the circle taking us past Taksim's hotel belt and down to the Golden Horn Bridge.

"Where you from?"

The usual exchange about England ensues. What we do. Where we live. Politely ask how long he's been in the taxi business and the conversation lurches into the bizarre.

"Always I drive. I work for a lawyer like you. A judge. Then go to prison." Makes a gesture with crossed wrists over the steering wheel. "Stab a man." Mimics a knife thrust concluding with a nasty twist of the wrist. "He on oxygen twenty days and I...fifteen years prison. Ten with discount." He makes the sentence sound disproportionately harsh for the crime in his eyes. "Anyway I know police so now I drive taxi."

The cab suddenly strikes me as over-warm. Stifling. The way Turks seem to like things. As though they're so afraid they might catch a chill that many of them wear jackets and jumpers on even the warmest of spring days.

"Is it okay to open the window?"

"Sure. Of course. You like smoking, drinking, fucking in the back. Is no problem."

Stunned silence. Alicia hisses "Did he really just say that?"

"I heard exactly what you heard."

Our driver carries on regardless. Points out the Iranian Consulate. Spits the name, Khamenei, like a curse. Laughs. Starts in on the Kurds and Barzani's visit to the President. "Big protest. Six thousand people. See the fences. Police vans." Points across at a pair of white painted armoured cars by the roadside. "We get here in time. Road will close soon." The traffic is indeed heavy and forward motion is stop-start. He forces the taxi into the smallest of gaps, makes liberal use of the horn and we make some progress over the bridge and along the embankment. "Rambo! Me Rambo!" he says with considerable relish as a less adventurous motorist loses his nerve and lets him past. Uphill into Sultanahmet. A few hundred yards from our destination when forward momentum stops.

"Is bad. Get out here."

Alicia opens the door and hops onto the pavement.

"How much do we owe you?"

A finger indicates the meter. "Sixty-two lira."

Hand him sixty-five. He looks down in disbelief. It's a good act. He fans out the three notes. "You make mistake." He's holding a ten and two fives. There's no sign of the fifty lira note I'm certain I gave him with a ten and a five. And I get it. The persona he's been so careful to convey. Of a nasty piece of work, with all the right friends. Prone to violence. And what am I going to do about this affront? This scam? A blaze of anger offset by a burst of desire to be out of this car into fresh air. Fight or flight? The dousing effect of common-sense takes over. He passes back a five lira note. I pull out another fifty as he clicks his fingers impatiently. Hand it across. Get out of the taxi carefully. My legs are slightly wobbly and I stumble at the kerb. Watch him edge away into the traffic. Sketch an ironic wave to him. No smile though. Just a glower.

"What's the matter?"

Tell Alicia what just happened. She takes my arm. "It's only about fifteen quid? We can afford it. She wraps herself around me, defusing the tension and starts to laugh as she kisses me. "Hey" she says. "It's a great story to have up our sleeves. The taxi-driver from hell. And nobody'll believe that could all happen in one short ride."

She's right of course. "Okay. Come on. I need a drink."

"Good plan, soldier."

Arms round each other we cross to the nearest cafe. Slump into chairs and the young waiter says "You okay? What can I get you?"

Tell him what just occurred. "Ah. The old money switch. It happens. My advice. Never pay until you get your bags out of taxi. Then if it's a trick, you can walk away. I get you something. A drink on me." And brings us cold glasses of wine. After which the scam doesn't seem to matter much anymore. Buy and sip refills. Tip the waiter handsomely when we leave for his kindness. It's all just life isn't it?

"What are we going to do tomorrow?"

Open the guidebook on the table in front of me. "Plenty of museums and art galleries. Topkapi. The military museum up at Osmanbey. Or there's Istanbul Modern."

"No way. We're going shopping. Where are the best shops?"

Consult the oracle. "Taksim according to this."

"Taksim it is then."

Meaning more walking. More spending.

***

The city we're exploring isn't pretty despite its history and the startling nature of some of its sights. It's gritty, dirty and very real. Its attraction is its life and its colour. Its smells and its warmth. Its vibrancy. Istanbul's denizens won't let you stand apart. They pull you in. Forcing greetings and smiles on you. Shaking your hand or cursing you. And if they do all this to sell anything and everything to you, then their motive is honest and understandable. To make a living from all they have.

It's a city which demands interaction. It wants you to answer back. To banter and joke. To forget your native reserve. To haggle. To repel its over-thrusting costermongers and to insult those who insult you. It will get under your skin. It will own your heart. An advertising brand on a tee-shirt says of Istanbul *They call it chaos. We call it home.* And that's what it's trying to become. Our second chosen home. Because unsurprisingly Alicia and I are falling in love with this city. And each passing day here we're more in love with each other. Or I think we are.

With time we come to recognise the faces of the owners and waiters from each bar and restaurant in the vicinity of our hotel. The cafe barkers claiming kinship with you on the basis of some nebulous connection with Palmers Green or Sutton Coldfield. Seeing the same beggars and street-sellers; the little girl with the beseeching smile and her armload of flower headdresses; the blind man with his white cane and the helper with the stack of artfully folded tea-towels for sale and the self-appointed guides who keep asking the same question of each passer-by; "What you look for? I help you." For a fee of course. Learn the art of slow progress and adamant refusal or the fast and purposeful walk which brooks no interruption. There is no middle way. We do both. As and whenever necessary.

On our last day Alicia says what I'm thinking. At a cafe near The Galata Tower. "Do we have to go home? I want to stay here forever. Like this. With you."

"Me too. Hold her hand across the table, playing with her fingers. "I think we should go back to the hotel and rest. Have a fabulous meal and too much to drink at Rumeli's tonight. Not even think about packing till the morning."

"Okay, soldier."

Lean in close and whisper in her ear. "Good because I've got plans for you."

"What plans would those be?" And she does this thing where she lightly bites her lower lip. Drives me crazy.

"It involves a comfortable bed and no clothes and..."

"I'm sorry. You'll have to be plainer. I'm not sure what you want."

"I want to fuck you."

Outburst of laughter. "Why didn't you say so? Come on. We're going." And I don't know who pulls who down the hill to the Karakoy tram-stop but we get there in record time.

***

This week I've learned one of the secrets of living life as it's meant to be lived. Full steam ahead. Take the ride to Istanbul with a fine woman. Spend twelve hours a day exploring the city, its backstreets, roof gardens, restaurants, bazaars, bars, mosques and fortifications and as much of the rest of your time as you can manage making love. Sleep? Who needs sleep? Siestas in the early afternoon heat, Turkish coffee sipped from ceramic thimbles and brandy are all you really need. The rest comes easy. Eventually you reach the condition caused by the combination of lack of sleep, too much caffeine and exhilaration in which the whole world feels completely unreal. Your head floats. Your limbs feel cold but your face is flushed. You'll be shivering in a minute. But, all in all, it's wonderful. Provided you don't mind returning to England bushwhacked and bleary-eyed. Actually bushwhacked is an Australian word meaning something else entirely. I mean bushed or whacked. Either or both.

One odd thing I can't explain. When we come to pack on our last morning, find we need to buy another case for the return trip. I mean I know we've bought a wall hanging, the piece of Suzani, but that rolls up pretty compactly. I just wasn't really aware that in five days we'd got all the items of new clothing and shoes we appear to have acquired. Immediate consequences, a few quid for excess baggage. What the hell? It's just that we seem to have spent money like water without even being aware of it.

Turkish Airlines flight blah blah blah departs five minutes ahead of schedule. We're on it. Sitting thoughtfully in row 25E and 25F, Alicia by the window holding my hand and dozing most of the way while I watch the in-flight movie without plugging in the headphones. Five hours later and we're at Birmingham, reunited with my car and setting off back to Lincoln. In some surreal translocation in another twelve hours we have to be at work again.

CHAPTER V: JUNE TO JULY

Contradictory weather. Heavy cloud. Scent of thunder in the air. No rain. Yet.

The real bugger is having to go back to work on Monday morning.

Jane wordlessly fetches me a well-sugared black coffee and then the diary. Letting me know I'm back in the real world with a price to pay for a week's leisure. People to catch up with, the papers for the forthcoming cycle of council meetings to sign off on and a file of reports and correspondence to deal with. I'll sift through most of that in due course.

Neil is in my office by ten o'clock complaining about the photocopier in the member's room. When am I going to get it replaced? Such minutiae surround and obfuscate the important strategic issues which constitute daily life in public sector management. Mind you this one I can pass on to Jane who in turn will palm it off on the admin officer. *Sort this for the Chief Executive right now please.* Request as three-line whip.

Eventually find the print-out of an email, red flagged under the post-it note. Jane's developing an enhanced sense of humour. It reads *Guaranteed to annoy, infuriate and worry.* The email is a memorandum from Simon Thornton, Director of Housing.

Disciplinary proceedings have resulted in the dismissal of three operatives for theft. No admissions were made nor any information provided that might make recovery possible of the missing school of Adams fireplace and surround. As Human Resources will confirm, rights of appeal against dismissal can be exercised within ten days and according to the union this will be done. An appeal suspends the dismissal so the employees remain on the payroll until the appeal is resolved. The council's normal practice is not to involve the police until the internal processes are concluded because criminal investigation enables the union to stonewall them so their members have to be paid until convicted. Do you concur?

Bit verbose. Could summarise simply as *Can't find the fireplace but sacked them anyway. Won't be involving the police until after appeal heard. Are you ok with that?*

And I'm not okay with that. It's preposterous, administrative bullshit. This is the sort of thing we should be prepared to fight even Unison and the GMB over. "Jane, get me Simon. And who's on the Disciplinary Appeals Sub-Committee?"

That shit apart, I can't take anything else on my desk seriously. And I don't know how to get through the day without phoning Alicia and letting her know just how stupidly much I'm missing being with her. Even though only two floors and a couple of corridors separate us, it feels like she's on the other side of the world.

Succumb early afternoon. "Are you coming over later?" Try and say it in as even a tone as I can manage. Don't want to seem too needy.

Brief heart-stopping silence before she says "I'm really tired. And I've got to check on everything the builders have done. And I need to unpack. How about tomorrow night?"

"Alright." Damn. What's up? Hardly a convincing set of excuses.

The trouble then is that the things we have to do; the things which get us through the day; those things don't matter at all. Not compared to the one we love. And when Alicia's not there I can't even be angry with her. She can't help being who and what she is. And she has a reason for not wanting to stay over at my house tonight. My frustration is not understanding what it is.

***

Screaming headlines on the billboards even I can't miss. Pick up copies of The Times and the Lincolnshire Echo. Between them they paint a horribly detailed portrait of the vivid underbelly of my city and the trials and tribulations of somebody's wife, caught up in it all, who's ended up in hospital. And the name Lenahan stands out amid the mass of newsprint. Not a common name. Of course it's the soccer star's family. The story's obviously going to run and run. A picture of a man draws my attention. It's not a good likeness but there's something familiar about the face. And then I remember him. He's Councillor Ross's ex-son-in-law. The man he asked me to meet soon after I started at the Council. The caption underneath springs another surprise. He's Clare James' brother. This is an incestuously small city.

Read the inside pages carefully. No mention yet of council department corruption. But that'll come sooner or later. You can bet your bottom dollar.

The day does what days like this do. Gets tougher as it goes along. And sometimes even professional courtesy doesn't help much. This time a phone call from Clare to warn me they're going ahead and arresting two of my planning officers. Hardly a shock given that the man who allegedly bribed them is already in custody but more problems to manage. Unsurprisingly Clare doesn't want to talk about her brother's predicament.

Ring the leader for a *Hey, Neil. You need to know* sort of conversation. Then my Head of Communications to work up a statement for the local media.

It doesn't take long before I'm delivering the statement to a an Echo reporter and agreeing to be interviewed by Yorkshire Television. Don't get to do the interview until I've taken a call from Dougie, a colleague who heads up a larger authority, trying to get dates for our action learning set's next meeting.

"Bit up to my ears in negative publicity at the moment."

"Why? What've you been up to?"

"It's nothing I've done. Couple of staff arrested on corruption charges. Local media are all over it naturally. Trouble is not much to say in our defence except we helped root out the problem."

"Could be worse. We had a gardener who murdered his partner. And all the cabinet member for leisure could think to say when asked to comment was how popular he'd been with the public and how amazing his flowers were. Shame he'd planted the girlfriend under one of the rose-beds."

Have to laugh. Puts my problems in perspective.

***

Doesn't matter how much fretting I do, things won't seem to settle back to normal. Even though in a day or two. Alicia resumes her regular occupation of the left-hand side of my king-sized bed, and work picks up where it left off. Interrupted admittedly by the bow-waves created by the ongoing police investigation into council which employs me to run a steady ship. But joy of joys no sightings of Darryl. By me anyway. Unfortunately Alicia's mood remains thoughtful and distant and I don't know what to do or say to put things right.

It doesn't help that I can't help thinking about the existence of an ex-husband somewhere on the planet. Try dosing her with wine one night to get some truth out of her. What I get are hints and only hints. "He was abusive. He left me in the end, thank God." None of which begins to address the issues I have with not knowing.

The one unfettered delight is that Alicia's house hits the market in mid-June and sells in short order not far off the asking price so she's making a quick turnaround profit of forty grand. It ought to sort out her finances once and for all. And she's already got her eyes on her next project. A mid-terraced town house. Three storeys. Ideal for student lets if the conversion's done right. If her offer's accepted, she wants to bridge any delay with a bank loan - after holding off completion as long as possible while she applies for an improvement grant to start work on it as soon as ownership passes.

And in the meantime we have to celebrate apparently. I'd settle for champagne and a good dinner but for her having that much money coming in seems to afford her broader spending temptations. New designer dresses; a wickedly expensive handbag, a jacket she insists on getting me; and her suggestion that we book a skiing holiday for next year – something she's always wanted to try apparently. And then she starts looking at new cars.

"Can you afford one now?" A key question if ever there was one.

"Probably not just yet. Let's go into Nottingham. I need some shoes." Smart heels for work and winter boots it appears.

But the restaurant's on me. Tonight I'm neither thinking about calories, weight gain nor training. Just goats cheese roulade followed by fillet steak. Different starter for Alicia but she's also on the red meat and fries.

"I can't do a dessert. No room. But you have one."

Shakes her head. "Coffee. And a liqueur."

"Sounds good." And it is.

Back to mine.

Where the sex is something else. Didn't think it could get any better. I was wrong.

***

Wake early. With a broad grin on my face and entirely predictable stirrings lower down. Pull her in to kiss her. Her lips are soft and her breath sweeter than I deserve.

"Umm...You can do that some more."

"So can you. And where are you going now?"

"Like Vasco de Gama, I'm heading South."

Laugh out loud. Have to. Only she could have come up with that. Don't think we'll be going to church this morning.

***

Disciplinaries and appeals. Tedious, legalistic, pedantic hearings in which everything has to be conducted just so in case we end up in a tribunal and some over-privileged chairman takes the view that as the public sector, we have a greater responsibility than any other employer. Whatever the law says. And then I can just imagine him; it has to be a him; sitting down with his cronies complaining about the inefficiency of local government, the cost of council services and the inexorable rise in council tax for less and less services year on year.

And this particular appeal is worse than usual because it could so easily be cut and dried. There's a written instruction regarding fixtures and fittings. It was ignored by the crew allocated the work. They were seen in the act of removing a valuable historical artefact which was never delivered back into council stores. And the person who caught them was somebody of good character and a county councillor to boot.

So I have to sit advising the Disciplinary Appeals Sub-Committee and re-hearing all the evidence with the trade union calling my Director of Housing a martinet and the punishment an excessive abuse of power. Personally I'd sack the lot of them for wasting my time sitting though this crap. But of course the offenders are on full pay for as long as they can spin it out. And there's no incentive to resign until the bitter end.

Early indications of trouble ahead with Janice Valency's evidence. Or more accurately, with her cross-examination by the union's solicitor.

"Are you sure these three men are the men you saw removing the fire place?"

"Yes. I'm sure."

"Then we need to go through your statement in more detail. Pages twenty-six to thirty in the bundle, I believe. You describe a conversation you had with the man in charge of the work at the house. The man the Director of Housing says was Martin Gibbs."

"Yes."

"And you say he was wearing a leather jacket over a council tee-shirt."

"Yes."

"And he had longish dark hair. Over his collar. And a full beard."

"Yes."

"That doesn't sound at all like Martin Gibbs." He gestures at a neatly turned-out man in a grey suit and blue tie. A clean-shaven man with a crew cut.

"That wasn't what he looked like then."

And of course it wasn't. We'll have to call evidence to the effect that he turned up at work two days after the theft once questions were being asked with a radical transformation of personal grooming and work attire.

"Or perhaps you just got the wrong man?"

"I didn't. I'd still recognise him. Even without the hair." Good answer.

"Right. Let's turn to Frank Jones. You described him as sandy-haired and bit overweight. I'll give you that. But you said he was average height. Can you stand up please, Mr Jones."

He does as he's told. We can all see he's around my height. Over six feet.

"The average height for men in the UK, depending upon which statistics you refer to, is around five foot nine inches. Mr Jones is six feet one and a half inches tall. I put it to you that you're mistaken about him too, Miss Valency."

"I'm not. I can explain that."

"Please try. By all means." Dripping with sarcasm.

"I'm quite tall for a woman and my boyfriend is really tall. Six foot four. Compared to him this man looked pretty average to me when I saw him on the street."

"Oh really. And what about the third man you saw? You didn't describe him in much detail at all. Did you? Just that he was dark-skinned and Asian looking. Are you a racist, Miss Valency?"

"No." In how she spits out that one word answer I can hear exactly how much she resents the suggestion.

"I checked and there are at least two other workers in the housing group from the Indian sub-continent. How can you be sure you got the right one?"

"Because I recognise him. They don't all look the same you know." And with that angry retort, she's lost it. And lost us the case. The impartiality of her evidence and her obvious good sense gone out the window.

Ian Porterfield tries his best to repair the damage. Calling his rebuttal evidence. Dealing with the workforce composition issue. Taking members through the task allocation records in the housing department which the union's solicitor has described as being of dubious accuracy.

None of it's enough.

The panel rises and takes an hour over coffee to reach a decision. Despite my best attempts to persuade them otherwise there's something happening in this room I can't put my finger on. A false undercurrent driving them to come back and uphold the appeal. *Reasonable doubt over the identification evidence.* Transparent rubbish. You'd laugh if it wasn't so manifestly absurd and damaging to the council's credibility to keep those three men on.

I like to think I don't readily show my emotions in a work situation. But right now I don't trust myself to engage in small talk with the panel members. Slap my papers together and stalk out. They probably know exactly where I'm going. And what short shrift I'll get there.

Neil's office. He takes one look at my face. "I can guess."

"Do you know how angry I am?"

"Uh-huh. But let me explain some facts of life to you. You had a balanced panel of five members. Three of them Conservative. You know my overall majority on the Council is down to four. I need all the support I can get so I'm not going to attack any of them even though I know they made the wrong decision. The other element you may not be aware of is that two of them are in the Lodge. As is one of the Labour members. The same Lodge to which Martin Gibbs belongs. Oh - and to complete the picture your other Labour member, Councillor Oakes, is a former Unison shop steward. I'd say it would always have been an uphill fight to beat that lot."

"And there's nothing I can do about it?"

Neil shakes his head. Frowning. "No. Let it go."

"The Director of Housing's already threatening to resign over it."

"He'll think better of it in the morning. Go home early. Simmer as much as you want. Have a beer or two. And then, as I said, let it go. This is Lincoln."

Unfortunately.

***

I know Neil's advice is rational given the odds. But I can't let it alone. Even if I wanted to. Not with Alicia's cousin round my house that evening having a real go. "They're in the same party as me for God's sake. And yet they're saying I'm an idiot. Or a liar. Just because I'm not in the funny handshakes club. I've a good mind to chuck the party whip and go to the bloody papers."

"You're not alone. Simon Thornton's saying he'll resign over this too."

Alicia keeps silent through all this. Making tea for us. Sitting on the settee beside me touching my arm as Janice and I argue. And then she's had enough. "Stop it the pair of you. It's like they used to say in Chicago. *You can't beat City Hall.* You won't win this battle. There'll be another fight along in a bit you can win. You have to wait for that one."

She's right of course but it doesn't stop Janice doing exactly what she threatened to do. Going into County Hall next morning and resigning from the Conservative party. Meaning her political career's over next May with the all-out county council elections. And she's still threatening to spill the beans to a local journalist. Like that's going to do us all the world of good. I think not.

Worse still I've got a bloody revolt on my hands. Would've been easier in some ways if Simon had resigned and I'd only got the wretched task of trying to find and appoint a new Director of Housing. Instead I've got an ultimatum on my desk. *Redeploy Martin Gibbs or else! No way we'll have him back in Housing.* In his shoes I might feel the same way. I don't want him anywhere in my organisation. But I don't have a choice thanks to the appeal fiasco. This one's going to run and run.

***

The one person I find I can talk that lot over with is Patrick. Meet him for a drink after work in town and he persuades me that Alicia's right. "Drop it. That's truly the only thing to do now."

Deep in thought leaving the pub I walk straight into an ambush of sorts. Darryl up close and viciously personal. No warning of the roadhouse swing at my head. The briefest glimpse of a moving shadow at the corner of my vision. Instinctively ducking. Perhaps he's been drinking because his timing's rubbish. His fist slams into the lintel. Just where my nose would have been. The howl of hurt is his. Push past him as he clutches his knuckles into his belly.

But something in me won't let this opportunity pass. Almost without thinking I'm swivelling to deliver the reverse kick we used to practice so regularly over and over. Thai kick boxing masquerading as keep-fit. Or vice versa. An accelerating foot crunching into the side of his knee. He goes down soundlessly. I know that feeling when the pain completely overwhelms the vocal chords and you can't even scream. I almost feel sorry for him. It doesn't last. Perhaps I should have aimed higher and permanently curbed any romantic intentions he might still harbour towards Alicia. Or higher still as he crumpled and smashed his pretty face in.

Walk away. Not hurrying. No need.

CHAPTER VI: JULY TO AUGUST

Dump Saul's car on a verge near Bolton Abbey. Been warned about the ridiculous price of official car-parking round here.

Not got the complete team today. Still waiting to be introduced to Saul's friends Steve, the fourth member of our quartet and Matt who's volunteered to be our driver. So it's just three of us, Saul, me and Alex. I already know him from the gym. Plus moral support in the shape of Alicia and Jess.

Trainers off. Walking boots on. For me brand new lightweight replacements for the heavily scuffed monstrosities originally bought for a sixth form geography field trip. A lot of years ago.

Get the rucksacks out. We're making some attempt to get used to carrying what we'll need when we do this for real up and down actual mountains. Fleeces. Rainwear. Water bottles. Sandwiches. Chocolate. The girls are exempt from being pack-mules. Saul and I have extra provisions for them.

The briefing at the foot of Simon's Seat is succinct. "Don't push it. We're just testing fitness levels today. And don't step on any ecto-thermic animals."

"Sorry, Saul. What're they, when they're at home?"

"Snakes. Specifically today - Adders. Stomp about and they'll disappear. They're more scared of you..."

"I can't stand snakes." Jess revealing a phobia we didn't know she had.

"Why not?" says Saul. "You're so matter of fact about spiders and mice. Even rats."

"Well they're not quite human are they?" Somewhere there's some female logic in that. And we do remember to be careful not to disturb any basking snakes.

Set off down the lane, diverting onto the footpath. Across fields. Over stiles. Ignoring the siren lure of strategically placed wooden benches. Want to see if we can do five miles without stopping. Or without an extended break anyway. Even though it gets steeper and stonier underfoot as we go higher and find ourselves following the natural lines of almost dry water-courses.

I'm puffing more than a little as we climb. Hard to catch my breath. Cardio-vascular fitness obviously an issue. Due to all the sedentary hours spent behind a desk. Mental note to tackle that with my trainer at the gym. The trouble with mountain and fell-walking is that the motions of climbing and descending are tough on knees and ankles. It's different to running and every muscle in my legs is cramping after the first serious pull uphill. And the infuriating thing is that Alicia, only along for the ride, dances through the arduous day with little by way of apparent ill-effects. I could cuff her in exasperation were it not for the ease with which she makes me laugh at myself and forget my aches and pains. Anyway she's directly in front of me most of the time and the view takes my mind off my exertions to some degree.

The last section up to the top of the ridge is a long haul which never lets up. And when you get there what's facing you is a pile of massive rocks to be scaled before you can say you're really done it. All for the joy of standing exposed to the four winds on a narrow little plateau. But the countryside beneath a cloudless sky is magnificent.

An unabashed Alicia puts her arms round me and kisses me. An even better outcome than the view to my mind. Kiss her back with gusto, ignoring Alex gurning away for my benefit. Silly sod.

"You can see half the world from here." Slight exaggeration but we know what Jess means, her blonde hair whipping around her face. Worth all the effort expended on getting here. Break out the water and chocolate. A lavish feast at this moment.

"We'd have made better time with walking poles of course." Saul checking his watch. Adding another item to my mental shopping list.

Going back down isn't too bad. Oddly the others all agree that downhill is harder than they thought it would be. Maybe the reason I don't think so is because it's much easier on my lungs.

Another good thing. Not a hint of a blister from my new boots. Game on.

Apart from the need for walking poles, we learn one other thing. It takes far too long to get our packs off and root round in them whenever we want to get a drink. Precious minutes lost every time.

Alex thoughtfully provides an answer. "We need those bladder things you can fill up and stick in your rucksack with a drinking tube sticking out. Save all that messing about."

"Yeah. You're right. One for the list, Saul."

"Certainly is."

"I'll have a look in town on my lunch-break tomorrow." Trust Alicia to get involved when there's shopping to be done. "We need four. One for each of you. Right?" Saves one of us having to get them.

After all the rigours of a day in Yorkshire, Alicia makes amends for her teasing my state of health by running a hot bath for me back at my house and taking me to bed straight afterwards. I hadn't thought I'd find the energy for that ever again but from somewhere...with what she does to me...

"Again?" A teasing hand working across my over-taut stomach muscles.

"You've gotta be kidding."

"Uh...no." Nibbling kisses along my jaw. Her mouth reaches mine. Resistance, such as it is...fleeting.

***

Wake curled into her sleeping form. Her breathing deep and regular. My hand rises of its own volition across her shoulder and into her thick mass of hair. My fingers separate silky strands, releasing residual hints of her shampoo to nuzzle. A peculiar sensation materialises. Unfamiliar for far too long. Being happy. A gurgling laugh. My own.

***

More bloody meetings. My life is full of meetings. Some local. Some further afield. Today it's London with the prospect of another day away from the office later in the week. That'll be a trip across to Warwick for the regional gathering of local authority chief executives.

Rise early to zoom down almost empty roads to Newark Northgate Station. Park up and get on the mainline service straight into Kings Cross. Sort through my notes before taking the luxury of reading the newspaper cover to cover. The train runs slightly late so even manage to finish the quick crossword. Result.

London in the morning rush hour in February's much what it always seems to be. Smelly and crowded with a clinging dampness in the air. The only compensation for the keen observer of the human condition is the unique range of characteristics of its denizens as they go about their business. Paradise for people watching in other words.

The tube's a case in point. It's full of interesting passers-by. The woman carrying a large wedding cake, each tier in its own individually-sized square Tupperware container, the boxes loosely strung together and hanging from a wire handle. Gerry-rigged. God help her if the stack slips and topples over. The elderly man with close-cropped grey hair topped by a low Mohican. The effect offset by horn-rimmed glasses and a hearing aid. Dotted around the carriage, flat caps are two a penny. Are they in vogue again? There's a gaggle of young Japanese girls. Probably older than their neo-fetishistic, schoolgirl attire suggests. One of them topping things off with a bowler. Old hat or new wave? You tell me. And English girls in short skirts and leggings with too much make-up for their actual age. Discussing shopping brands and boys in no particular order of importance. Two Sikhs conversing in low tones, their faces no more than an inch or two apart. Both black and white students carrying engineering textbooks and large folders of drawings. Any aspiring writer could get a good story out of any one of them. Just haunt the Circle Line or sit and people watch in an art gallery. All life is to be found down here in the smoke if you want it.

I just want to get off at the right stop. The Temple. I've come for a so-called con with the council's barrister. That's con as in consultation not as in scam. Although with the level of fees we're paying...

Geoffrey Evans QC is highly dubious about the council's chances in the judicial review proceedings we're facing. Suggests we settle. Does so with a serious frown intended to convey gravitas. Unnecessary. His logical analysis is good enough for me.

"I'll try and persuade the leader. Can you send me a beefed-up legal opinion?"

"Right-o."

Go home. A waste of a day but if Neil Wetton agrees we won't spend any more time and energy on this matter.

Alicia's out when I get home. A note to say she's working on her house if I want to join her. Changing into jeans to do just that when the bell rings. Find Janice standing on the doorstep. Tell her where Alicia is but encourage her in for a glass of wine. See if I can take advantage of this unforeseen opportunity to loosen her tongue because I can't think of anybody else who might be willing to tell me anything about the bastard Alicia used to be married to.

She doesn't want to respond to my inquiry but she's far too polite to try to fob me off completely.

"You need to ask Alicia. It's not my place..."

"She won't. So you have to. I have to know what I'm dealing with."

"You know he was a sod to her?"

"Yep."

"And in the end, he pushed her too far and she put him in hospital."

"No! What do you mean?"

"You have to talk to her. That's all I'm saying."

"You can't leave it there. You just can't."

"I can say he deserved it. And they got divorced and she was well shot of him."

And, despite my urgings, she won't say another word on the matter. When she's gone, I find I've lost any urge I might have had earlier to play builder's labourer for what's left of the evening.

***

The human resources lot get nowhere with redeploying Martin Gibbs. He phones wanting an appointment with me.

It's a fair while since the disciplinary appeal and already he more closely resembles Janice Valency's original description. There's no sign of the smart suit and his hair and beard haven't seen the clippers in weeks.

Get Jane to make him a coffee and sit him down in the outer office with a standard council job application form. "There's a bit of a problem with your personal file. Can't find your original forms from back when you first got the job here. That seems to be why they're having problems finding suitable redeployment for you. So just fill this in with all your details and we'll have another go."

A knock on my door half an hour later. When I shout "Come in" Gibbs appears in the doorway. "How've you got on?" He looks nervous. There's a line of sweat across his forehead. I'm not used to inspiring fear to this degree.

"It's a bit difficult to remember everything." He's clutching the form to his chest in a very odd manner. "Perhaps I should take it away now and get it back to you when it's filled in."

"How far have you got?" Stand up and put my hand out so he has no choice but to hand me the form. In a spidery hand he's written his name at the top. Apart from that it's blank.

And this is a man who's been employed by us to submit professional reports and manage a technical work group. But who on earth gave him the job? Covered for him? Because the only obvious explanation I can see for the sheet of paper in my hand is that this man can neither read nor write.

***

The signs foretelling troubled water ahead keep on coming. Tuesday night. The now regular pub quiz. Patrick Butler taking me aside to tell me something.

"Look I feel a bit disloyal saying this but watch out with Alicia."

"What are you saying?"

"She's a bit over-extended I'd say. With the house purchases and everything."

"Houses in the plural?"

"Two more that I know of and I'm beginning to wonder if she's got her fingers in any other pies. Are you ok with where she's at?"

Say I am. But in truth I didn't even know. But what the hell can I do about it? This is a woman who can't even bring herself to talk to me about her former marriage. Never mind the vexed subject of money. Haven't a clue how to react to Patrick's well-meant advice. However much I rack my brains over it.

***

For administrative convenience the heart of England falls to be divided into east and west. Not much sense in the split. I mean Leicester's closer to Coventry than it is to Lincoln and there's plenty of strong links across the notional boundaries. Nevertheless the East Midlands Chief Executives meet together regularly, as do their West Midlands counterparts but the whole lot only come together once in a blue moon to review regional matters and to exercise their communal prejudices against the South-East. Which really in this context means Greater London. Leaving Kent and Sussex irrelevantly beyond the pale.

As isn't unusual with infrequent meetings, the agenda for Warwick's gathering is lengthy. Not to say dull. And with financial inequalities a key issue, the mood can best be described as griping in tone. I get touches of deja-vu all day. We used to have the mirror image of the self-same discussions about the Inner London Boroughs when I worked down South.

There's no lunch-break as such. We munch sandwiches on the hoof, still only halfway through the business of the day. Exceedingly glad when things break up late afternoon. And then it's like a Le Mans start with them all racing for their cars, elbows pumping and the devil take the hindmost. Suspect they'll hit the motorways just as rush-hour builds and they'll be crawling along in traffic jams for the most part. I prefer the notion of a lazy cappuccino and the seductive temptation of a chocolate muffin.

Head out of Shire Hall into the market square, past the old boxer, Randolph Adolphus Turpin. He's showing none of the agility that once made him middleweight champion of the world. But then again few statues step out to throw any new shapes at all in my experience and Randolph's no exception.

Change my mind about settling for coffee when I see the sign for cream teas in the window of a café run for charity. Fetching a smile from the middle-aged waitress. She replies "Yes dear" when I tell her what I'll have. Let the tea mash a few minutes. Reading the paper. No sign of my scones. Pick up the spoon to stir the tea. And find out my order's miscarried. She's given me Chinese tea. A green tea.

Set out for home chuckling inside. One to tell Alicia. If she's in evidence when I get home. My strategy in recent days has been to abandon any hope of tackling anything meaningful longer-term and to concentrate on the one area in which we seem to thrive.

She is home as it happens. And feeling playful. "I've got a bottle of white on ice in the bedroom. And strawberries. And chocolate..."

"Get up those stairs right now, girl."

"Race you."

She wins. Not by much of a margin. And only because I don't want to trample her in the mad rush and because I'm divesting layers of clothing as I go.

Much later lying flat out on the bed with the duvet bunched over our inter-twined legs she makes one of her characteristically off the wall observations. "You've got a pretty flat bottom. And I've got a bigger one than you." Not sure why that truth is suddenly pertinent.

"Yep." Could have denied it because hers really isn't big by any stretch of the imagination but her tone doesn't carry any hint of a need for reassurance.

"It's curvy bombalini,"

"Is that Italian?"

"No. I just made it up." As she does.

Lying there, trying to count my blessings with Alicia's head on my chest, realise gratefully that, since smacking him one, Darryl's been conspicuous by his absence anywhere in my line of sight. Wonder if she knows about the beating Darryl's taken from me. Hope she doesn't. Not sure whether it wouldn't push her sympathies a step or two in his direction. Consider asking her if there've been any emails. Decide not to raise it. Or anything else. Sleeping dogs can stay that way.

CHAPTER VII: AUGUST TO DECEMBER

It's hard not to like August. A month for catching up. No formal council meetings. The luxury of time to consider. To plan. To tour the outlying offices. Even visit the council crematorium. Where they demonstrate the process of burning a body and ensure I watch through the little viewing window into the cremator. Grisly stuff. Grinning staff. Part of the initiation of a new chief. The last guy was here donkey's years so I'll be the new kid on the block for a good while yet.

The trouble with having time and space for thinking lies in the old maxim about the devil and idle hands. Not mine of course but all the others slobbing around City Hall in the absence of their political masters. Even if they work hard most of the rest of the year. Vow to make August a more productive month next year.

Finish early each day. Could get used to this. Never got to be home at tea-time in London. Energy too for working on Alicia's latest project. The town house destined to be good quality student flats. I'm not supposed to be aware there may be other properties in Alicia's burgeoning portfolio so I don't let on what Patrick felt compelled to tell me.

"Grab that."

"What?"

"I mean can you take the other end of this please, honey." Pointing at a newly painted internal door leaning against a wall. Big smiles. Hers and mine.

***

Divorce, like war, is composed of two elements. Shorts bursts of activity, fascinating and scary, interspersed by long periods of stasis. It doesn't matter how much you want anything to change, it doesn't ever seem to happen overnight. Unless you feel like committing economic suicide, you have to keep going to work while you wait for the right moment to arrive. And the waiting is the hardest part. Boring but necessary. Like marking time until your best girl gets off work. But less exciting. A better comparison might be standing around in the cold, stamping your feet to keep warm, while your dog takes its time over doing its business in the park.

But it will happen in the end. Separation creates its own unstoppable dynamic. Get a welcome telephone call from Michael O'Suillibhain. Telling me to expect some paperwork he's forwarding from Marianne's solicitors. "Things are moving at last. We've agreed the grounds."

"They're not citing Alicia are they?"

"No. Unreasonable behaviour."

"So how much of a bastard do I have to agree I've been?"

Michael laughs. "Black-hearted. A pantomime grade villain. The price you pay. Good news is there are no other complications. So a fifty-fifty split as we discussed."

"Quicker the better. I'd like to reduce my mortgage and have a bit of cash to start work on my new place. If I leave it like this much longer, I'll stop noticing the holes in the plaster and just how crap the kitchen and bathroom are."

"She wants you to pay her legal costs of course."

"Is that normal? How much is that going to cost me?"

"It won't bankrupt you. I'll email you a draft fee account for my services and get you an estimate from her solicitors. I've only eaten into my retainer by about four grand so you shouldn't have to find much more." Fat comfort. He's had eight thousand out of my overdraft so far. Still if the end's in sight...

***

Another training walk. This time up Snowdon. Practising on the real thing. It's hard. Debate the joys of the different routes open to us but we'll have to do the steepest because it'll be much quicker. Bit weird to think next year we'll be climbing this after already doing Ben Nevis and Scafell Pike and however weary we are we'll need to do it, up and down, in around four hours.

The view from the top on a cloudless day repays the effort to get up there with the whole team. Even our co-opted driver, Matt, is with us in the group photograph. Saul's other friend Steve gels effortlessly with the rest of the team. A wiry little joker of a man who pushes us to go at things harder than we might. And Saul is right about one other thing. The descent's a lot easier with our new walking poles.

**

Back at work not everybody's brains are vegetating. Kevin Lewis, Head of Leisure, is pressing Jane for a slot in my diary. Agree he can have one. Plenty of spare time to fill.

"When you started here you told us you intended to shake this place up and change it for the better. And you asked us to think creatively and laterally. Did you mean it?"

"Of course."

"Then I've got a belter of an idea for you."

It is too. A madcap plan to charter a jumbo jet from British Airways, defray the cost by selling seats to Lincoln residents and fly it to Neustadt-an-der-Weinstrasse, our German twin town, for a day trip to Oktoberfest, the wine festival. A few problems of course. Like the fact that Neustadt hasn't got an airport. On the other hand we do have one at our end with a usefully long runway. It's called RAF Waddington. Who's going to be schmoozing the station commander now? Guess.

Starts as a bizarre conversation on the telephone. "If I hire a jumbo, can I fly it from your base?"

Odder still over a coffee, he says "Yes." What a star. "There are a few practical details." There would have to be wouldn't there?

"Thought that. Who do we need to talk to about resolving them?"

Back in the office give Kevin his head. "See if we can make it stack up. And mention to the Leader what we're up to."

Share the notion with Alicia when she gets home. She thinks it's ridiculous. So do I. But it just might happen anyway.

Quickly disabused of that possibility. Don't often start the day with a phone call from the Pentagon. To be honest, never. A softly spoken voice but one impossible to place as anything but American. Sounding just like someone out of a movie. But it's neither his accent nor his place of work which throw me.

"Look here, fella. We've been exercising our brains about your mayor's request to use our base at Rammstein to land your jet. Now I know one a'my forebears here let ya do it last time. He had clout. Three stars on his chest and all the attitude coming from bein' raised in Lincoln, Nebraska. Which your guys surely played on. But that was a long time ago and things have changed. Security an' all. So real sorry to be the bearer of bad tidings. But the answer's gonna be no."

"No room for manoeuvre then?" Thinking on my feet.

"Fraid not."

"Well it's very good of you to phone in person. Must be late at your end. And I really appreciate you considering it."

"A pleasure, sir. A real pleasure." Not quite sure how to take that as he hangs up. Whoever he was. Didn't catch his name. Jane's probably got it.

Several puzzling aspects about the conversation. One reference in particular.

"Jane, can you dig out the Neustadt twinning files. Going back say twenty years to start with. I need to look over some old history."

"Files that age'll be in the basement. I'll get them sent up. This afternoon all right?"

"Fine. No great rush. Do you know whether Councillor Ross was here back then?"

"He's been on the council a long time certainly."

"Then ring him and ask if I can have a word. Thanks."

"Will do."

"And I could murder another coffee."

***

Peter Ross is on the phone inside the hour, bless him. "What can I do for you?"

Explain the idea Kevin Lewis has come up with. "Has anything like this been done before, to your knowledge?"

"Certainly has. Must have been for the twenty-fifth or thirtieth anniversary of the twinning. They took a chartered plane over for some big event. I didn't go myself. But it was a pretty well received I believe."

"That helps nail it down. Thanks Peter."

"No trouble at all. See you at council." He means the next full council meeting. Nothing wrong with his memory. For the past or the immediate future.

The files confirm it was the thirtieth anniversary they were celebrating. And Jane finds a contemporary video from Yorkshire Television of the event and has a local photographic shop pull out all the stops to get it transferred onto DVD for me to watch in my office. To my eyes it clearly was a successful idea. Shame we can't replicate the experience now.

"Get Kevin Lewis up for me, please, Jane."

Power. He's up the stairs in less than ten minutes.

"Come in. How's the Oktoberfest idea shaping up?" Grossly unfair of me to play him rather than blasting him with both barrels.

"It's...it's coming along. But we have a problem with getting a landing slot at Frankfurt. It's such a busy airport. We're working on an alternative."

"The USAAF airfield at Rammstein?"

"Yes. That's right. How did you know that?"

"I had a very nice man from the Pentagon on the phone this morning. He said that a certain three star general probably had no right to authorise Rammstein's use twenty years ago and with current security considerations they won't be allowing it again. He said *no* very politely though."

"Oh." Kevin looks aghast.

"So tell me this. Why did you let me believe this was your original idea?."

"I'm sorry..."

At least he doesn't bluster or offer weak excuses. Or worse still try to deny the indefensible.

"Did you think I wouldn't find out? Well now it'll have to be scrapped. It isn't gonna fly." Can't resist that one. "Don't ever mislead me like that again. Now get out."

Jane taps and sticks her head round the open door. "You okay? He shot past my desk like a bat out of hell."

"Yeah. Just seething. Better get me the Leader. Need to tell him we won't be flying to Neustadt next month."

***

Galling end to another matter too. Sign off the compromise agreement terminating Martin Gibbs' employment with the council and compensating the undeserving son of a bitch with a cheque for fifty thousand pounds. For the privilege of getting rid of him. Crime obviously does pay. And not just for lawyers. I'd like to be able to take photocopies of that cheque and ram one down the throat of each and every one of the members of the Disciplinary Appeals Sub-Committee. Mind you that'd get me fired. Might be worth it though.

***

I was wrong about flying to Neustadt for Oktoberfest. By official invitation, seats on a scheduled flight to Frankfurt carrying civic gifts. Only two of us though. Neil and me. Dinner with the Oberburgermeister. Decent hotel. Trip up to the Hambacher Castle. Lunch. Speeches at the festival opening. A short one in English from Neil. Not too much use of local idiom to baffle the translator. Then we get hammered on too many tasting glasses of the innocuously deceptive new wine. And fly home the next morning with acute hangovers.

The mayor's chauffeur meets us at Birmingham International. Doze most of the way home. I'm dropped off at my front door. Alicia takes one look at me. Mutters disapprovingly and banishes me to bed. Sensible woman.

CHAPTER VIII: DECEMBER TO JANUARY

Alicia's approach to the holiday season borders on the schizophrenic. She loves Christmas but is depressed by the passing of another year and won't celebrate New Year's Eve except in bed with me. She hates tinsel but hangs colourful ribbons over the pictures on the wall in my bedroom. Contradictions abound. In a nutshell we celebrate Christmas no holds barred and ignore every New Year's Eve invitation that dares worm its way through our letterbox.

No sooner is the holiday week over than Alicia's focus switches to the sales. "It'll be a good time to get ourselves the stuff we'll need for Andorra." She went ahead and booked the ski trip straight after selling the student conversion. Just because her friend Julie is skiing-mad.

"What do we really need? Jackets and trousers. Not much else surely for beginners. We're hiring boots aren't we?"

"Socks. Ski socks." She waves a snow-sports magazine at me. "Helmets. We have to have helmets. And thermals. They've got these things called *Skins*. Really warm but they breathe so they're dead comfortable to wear. They don't get sweaty. Everybody's getting them."

Who's everybody? "Well we can probably get everything we need at Decathlon. In one trip." I mean the big sports warehouse chain. French I think.

"No way. I want a really cool ski-jacket. And a buff."

"What on earth's a buff?" Nearly came out with something else. Ruder. Restrain myself.

"It's a sort of circular scarf. Goes round your neck and you can pull it up over your nose and ears if it gets really cold. And there's no flapping end to catch on anything. And they come in all sorts of colours and designs."

How come somebody can get so excited about a buff? It's just a scarf. Or am I missing something?

"Oh. And we'll need goggles."

"Right. Is that the complete list then?"

"Lip block and sunscreen."

"For skiing?"

"Yep. If you don't want to get burnt. It says here the sun reflects back off all the snow and you can get your face burnt really easily."

"Oh." Sounds like another expensive shopping trip in the offing. Quietly resolve to resist temptation wherever we go and slip away to Decathlon for myself. Be quids in. Don't make the mistake of saying so to Alicia. All I need do is stonewall whatever we see in town or in Nottingham or wherever else we end up going.

As a tactic it doesn't work. First Alicia finds me a beautiful grey ski jacket. "The colour's fabulous for you and it's got a quilted inner back liner. It'll be so comfortable. And it's almost half price." How can you fight logic like that? It's still not exactly a giveaway but my credit card can cope.

Just as well I'm steeled. Alicia's jacket and salopettes are reduced by the merest fraction from an extortionate price. You're paying of course for the neat crawling spider logo. The very thing which should be putting her off. She can't stand creepy-crawlies in the house. Can't help gently reminding her she borders on arachno-phobia but I don't come anywhere near deterring her from completing the purchase.

"You need good ski socks." Alicia's next pronouncement. No discount on those. "Four pairs each for now." Bloody hell. Don't pay anything like this for other sports socks. Even my padded walking ones guaranteed for a thousand miles, and deemed more than adequate for the Three Peaks Challenge.

And I won't tell you what the goggles cost. Or the thermal layers. Or the silkily comfortable buffs. By comparison the helmets are almost bargains given their future role in our safety. So in the end the only bit of gear left to be purchased at Decathlon turns out to be my salopettes. Even have to arm-wrestle Alicia away from the displays of ski-boots. "We've already got hired boots and skis in the holiday package. Nearly slipped up there but at least the notion of buying her own skis doesn't seem to have crossed her mind.

Take all the bags and packages to my place and pile them up in the front room. Looking at the stack, we might need larger suitcases. Don't mention that to Alicia. She's in much too good a frame of mind from the trip to the sales. Feeling no guilt, she's exhibiting all the signs of becoming amorous and I have every intention of taking advantage as some compensation for my retail patience. An early night beckons.

***

After the seasonal break and our shopping extravaganza, we could be forgiven for allowing free rein to a touch of seasonally-affected depression. Except that before our skiing holiday there's the little matter of a giant-killing opportunity for Lincoln City FC.

Any FA Cup third round draw is likely to be both good news and bad, in equal proportions, for a lower division club. It's something of a miracle already to get this far and ideally the team would love to go even further in the competition. For reasons both reputational and financial. But there are no easy games at this point so getting a high profile team on your home turf in the draw is consolation indeed. It means a sell-out crowd howling for our side and a healthy boost to the club bank account. And on the right afternoon any professional team might hypothetically beat any other so you can't help hoping. Factor in that the match is an East Midlands derby and one which sees a former young hero return to his old stomping ground; the prolific goal-scorer, Rory Lenahan. It appears the rumours of his move to Ajax in the transfer window were just so-much journalistic codswallop. Instead he's now playing for a Leicester side well on its way to the Premiership title. And Lincoln drawing them looks a pretty cool outcome. Now if we only could beat them...

As Saturdays in early January go, it's not too cold but still more sensible to wear a jumper and quilted jacket than anything smarter. Alicia's not with me. Places in the council box at Sincil Bank are in short supply and luckily for peace and harmony she's not particularly into sport.

It's a couple of miles from my home to the ground and I could've had a lift with the leader in the mayoral car but choose to walk, enjoying the atmosphere on the streets. Shops and market stalls emblazoned in the team colours and lots of good-humoured banter among the strolling fans, tolerant of even those obviously here to support the opposition. But going to enjoy the football doesn't extinguish one marring factor. I'm examining the crowd half expecting to see Darryl at any moment. I don't. But that's no guarantee he's not going to be somewhere in the crowd.

Despite walking I still manage to get there early only to find everybody's had the same idea. Neil and a couple of other cabinet members are already holding court for a bunch of senior representatives of partner organisations, many of them vaguely familiar faces to me, even if I can't name all of them. Glad to see Clare among them, in mufti rather than uniform, smiling at me as she stands there beside a good-looking teenage lad. There's a tall bearded man with her too and I know him but can't place him in this company until Clare introduces him as her brother and of course I recognise him then. And remember where I've met him before and why. And precisely what to avoid talking about. That makes for carefully banal conversation.

"Hello. How's it going?" A good stopgap to hold things for a bit.

"Fine, thanks."

"Looking forward to the match?"

"Of course. Split loyalties though. I used to coach Rory. And he's engaged to my niece, Clare's girl."

A waitress from the catering company comes through with a tray of nibbles, allowing us to drift apart, removing any risk of me blurting out any embarrassing personal questions or unwanted expressions of sympathy.

Clare takes my arm and steers me towards the window. "They're coming out." Grab a glass of white wine for each of us as we slip past the side-table and after that get engaged in what we're supposedly here for, neither business nor politics, but a team in red and white trying to overcome blue-shirted opposition.

The third Leicester player out of the tunnel and onto the pitch is their number seven. He gets a bi-partisan roar of recognition. No hint of crowd hostility for his desertion from the ranks of the Imps. Surprisingly his popularity here is undiminished. Perhaps it's the transfer fee he brought in and the three new players it funded. None of which stops him playing at his lethal best and a valiant defence lasts un-breached barely thirty minutes. By half-time we're two-nil down, Lenahan scoring the first with a twenty yard volley into the top right hand corner of the net. Which secures a quickly suppressed squeal of excitement from his mother-in-law-to-be and admiring sighs from the rest of us. Though with an eye to past loyalties, Lenahan doesn't celebrate his goal. Just trots back to the centre-field for the re-start.

At the break, some of the guests head out to the bar for beers. Others focus on getting the plastic covers off the sandwiches and sausage rolls. Not much here for vegetarians. Doesn't worry the carnivore in me. Not at all. Munch some pretty special pork pie sourced from an excellent local butcher and lifting another glass of wine, find myself standing next to the teenager who was with Clare when I arrived.

"Hi. Enjoying the game?"

He's got a heaped plate of food and is in the act of biting off a big hunk of a ham roll just as I turn my attention to him. Splutters and swallows hard. Puts out his right hand to be shaken. Realises I'm holding both plate and glass and can't reciprocate. Pulls it back. Grins infectiously. "I'm Liam. Rory's my brother." Which makes him yet another of the apparently vast and criminally-tainted Lenahan clan. "It's great isn't it?" His excitement is patently obvious.

"Yes. Fantastic occasion. But your brother's in a different class, isn't he? Did you use to see him play for Lincoln much?"

"All the time. Dad used to bring me to watch..." A shadow flickers across his freckled features and he stumbles over his words before adding "Now we see him at the King Power Stadium. My brother says it's not like the Filbert Street days. But it's sponsorship innit. We got season tickets. Do you want to meet him? I can get you his autograph."

"That's a nice thought. My nephews collect autographs. They've got mostly cricketers so far. We were all staying at a family wedding one summer in Amsterdam a few years ago when they were small and we got up for breakfast and found most of the Australian, Pakistani and Indian national teams staying there for some competition or other. So we got them all to sign for us."

"I didn't know they played cricket in Holland."

"Mad about it apparently."

"Oh! I like cricket."

"Do you play?"

"Yes. For my school."

"Batsman or bowler?"

"Bit of both. I'm middle-order."

"And you enjoy the game?"

"Why wouldn't I?"

Clare interrupts. "Thanks for looking after Liam. They're starting again."

"Don't think he needed looking after. We just had a good chat."

Liam nods in agreement and it's back to the action.

It would have been good to get a consolation goal at least in the second half but that's not to be. We don't really get back into the match at all. And Leicester don't let up on us. The one highlight which transcends all rivalry is a brief demonstration of outrageous talent. Rory Lenahan racing down the left wing with the ball glued to his feet. Reaching the by-line. Side-stepping a defender and putting in the perfectly weighted cross so that all his strike partner has to do is rise enough to get his head to the ball and it's in the back of the net for three-nil. The audacity though isn't in the goal itself or even the accuracy of the cross but in the manner in which it's delivered. He projects it with his right foot wrapped behind the calf of his standing left leg.

Rory's former coach is the first person to break the silence in the box. "There's a name for that."

"You mean shit hot."

"It's called a rabona."

"Whatever it's called, it's pretty amazing."

The Leicester manager substitutes Rory Lenahan five minutes before the end. To gift him the standing ovation from the whole crowd which is so well-earned. Even if for the wrong side. And his younger brother bolts away downstairs to join him.

At the final whistle the guests thin out quickly. Take the time myself for a quick word with Neil. "A great day all round."

"Worked didn't it? And fantastic to have so many of our partners turn out."

"Certainly was. See you Monday."

"God willing." Till then wouldn't have said Neil had a religious bone in his body.

CHAPTER IX: JANUARY TO MAY

A sign says *Breakfast bap and pint £6*. Who'd want a beer at six-thirty in the morning? Plenty of people it appears. And not just the winter sun seekers. There are fit looking people in ski jackets in the bar imbibing too. So much for heading out for healthy exercise.

Some of the aircrew still wear high heels and glossy American tan tights. Not the Captain of course. My presumption anyway. She doesn't actually come out of the cockpit. After take-off the stewardesses change into flatties to save wear and tear on their legs and feet. A sane and sensible approach to a working life at twenty thousand feet plus.

The trip brings a disconcerting contrast. Wet and windy at home. Then delivered via hermetically sealed aircraft cabin and packed transfer coaches into deep snow and beautiful sunshine.

I've never stood on a mountain in proper snow before. Let alone skied on one. And it's nothing like the introductory course we did at Tamworth's Snowdome as some form of preparation. Standing here with planks of wood strapped to my feet is pretty scary stuff. Nervous tension palpable in every strand of my DNA. If it wasn't for an absolute determination to show no sign of weakness or fear in front of Alicia, I'd be considering abandonment. Instead I'm pushing off on a gentle slope trying desperately to turn my snowplough into the beginnings of a parallel turn. And if I don't want Alicia to see through me, I'm certainly praying that the instructors do. I want to be put in a class with other rank amateurs. I get my wish. One up for expert insight. And looks like I can progress at my own pace without adverse female commentary because Alicia's in the next group up the skill ladder. The first time in months I've been happy to be separated from her.

Next stroke of luck. Getting a very patient ski instructor who chivvies the ten of us along until we can all come down a short stretch of a green run without crossing our skis or falling over. It's tiring though and the stop for hot chocolate can't come soon enough. Nor lunch-time, an hour or so later when classes end and we all meet up. Got a hell of an appetite. End up scoffing a large plate of pasta and meat masquerading as some previously unlabelled or unclassifiable dish and polishing off Alicia's leftovers to boot. Finish off with a sugar hit and manage another hour's practise with Alicia and a couple of other keen souls. Culminating in a hair-raising, if painfully slow, slalom down a blue run to the town. We could have taken the gondola instead but common-sense is fleeting when sky-high levels of confidence kick in. Don't fall but survive a narrow squeak with a couple of dangerously self-centred snowboarders.

"We should do that exercise where you tie ski poles round your waist. Take out a few boarders if they come too close." Alicia preaching revenge in Fat Albert's Bar where we're watching clips of our respective groups in action, filmed using head-cam technology. Seems like most of our tour party are with us. The bar's jammed with bodies consuming extraordinary quantities of beer and wine. Roars whenever somebody spots a mate on the big screen. "There's you!" Alicia's elbow underlining the fact.

"Sure is." Actually I look alright. Some of the filmed victims are skiing sideways or even sitting down. I look okay by comparison.

Alicia agrees. "Hey! Not too shabby."

A few minutes later I watch her in action, putting me to shame. Admit as much.

"No" she says. "You did good for a first timer."

Actually I have to agree. It does feel good. Have another drink on the strength of it.

Back at the hotel sleep comes instantly and soundly. No call for birth control even though I packed condoms. Just in case.

***

Days Two through to Six pretty much replicate our first outing on the slopes. But with growing confidence on longer pistes. Our instructor keeps us well away from red and black runs and by the end of the week I'm enjoying myself enormously. I can see myself doing it again another year. That'd be cool. But there's what must be the usual crap at the end. Loading suitcases and ski bags into our coach's luggage bay at four in the morning. People climb aboard yawning or sighing with relief. The latter particularly true of parents with young children. Phil from my ski school group starts to hum.

"If you sing, I'm going to have to kill you."

A disembodied voice at the back offers support in depth. "You won't have to. I'll kill him first."

Eventually get on the road, rolling gently down the main street. Past the shops and hotels. Across a roundabout, picking up speed. A mood of diminished attention prevails and most passengers on the coach doze for the hour or two it takes to get as far as the comfort stop once we're over the French border.

No different to a week ago. A little cafe is the only thing open in the village. Apart from the pissoir down by the river. Twenty minutes queuing for a croissant and coffee or to use a proper toilet. Climbing back onto the bus, Alicia slides into the wide double seat, wads her ski jacket into a makeshift pillow, pounds it into the right shape against the window, settles down and falls asleep immediately. Little snorts erupt occasionally telling me the depth of her slumber and I move her gently around until I can put my arm round her shoulders and snuggle her onto my chest. All I can see of her now is the top of her head, the fantastical colour of her hair catching the half-light of early morning. Making me smile. And what I think about is running my fingers through it. And kissing her mouth. Not a bad recipe for travelling.

Toulouse is just an airport. Better than some. Fewer facilities than many others. The toilets clean but the duty free and eateries limited. But that's okay. We just want to be gone now. And in the banal normality of flying, we get there. Thankful and tired. To join another queue to be allowed back into Britain. To find my car and get home to Lincoln. Tumble through the front door. Dump the bags. Switch the heating on. Head for bed. Pulling off our clothes. Diving under the duvet. And sliding unceremoniously into sleep. It's going to take a few hours before dawning consciousness sets a new agenda. Making love. And then sharing a pot of tea at the kitchen table. The right order of business. The proper markers of homecoming.

***

Into the office early next day. Very early. A lot to catch up on. Leaving Alicia in bed. She doesn't need to be in till her first meeting at half past nine. Halfway through the pile of post marked important even before Jane gets in.

"Hi. You're keen today. Good holiday?"

"Yeah. It was."

"So you can ski now?"

"After a fashion. Not too many falls. No hurt pride. Certainly do it again."

"You've got some colour too."

"The weather was great. Lots of snow before we got there and we were learning in clear sunshine. Jackets open and just t-shirts. Didn't need those bloody expensive thermals Alicia insisted we get. Nor the goggles. Ended up buying new sunglasses."

"That's suntan on your face not dirt then?"

"Cheeky woman. Where's my coffee?"

"Putting me in my place, chief?"

"Of course. Have one with me and we'll go through what's urgent. Any problems for you while I was off?"

"No. It's been fine. Jack coped pretty well." She means my deputy of the moment. Each of the directors is doing a month in rotation covering for me whenever I'm away from City Hall. They know they can ring my mobile if they need me but it's good for all of them to see the full breadth of what happens and to test their brains a bit. Shift them out of their comfort zones. And the management team needs to develop. This is just one more way of doing it.

"Pencil him in for a de-brief then."

"Already in the diary."

"Brilliant." Genuine admiration. Known for ages she makes me look way more in control of this place than I really am.

Coffee comes with more paperwork. But actually no apparent crises. Next year I might manage two consecutive weeks off on leave.

The liquid residue in the bottom of my cup starts to ripple and the saucer vibrates. Wonder what's happening for a second. Realise my mobile's lying on the desk. On silent but going off. Pick it up quickly. It's Alicia.

"Hi, sweetness. What's up?"

A sharply indrawn breath. Close to distress. "I'm in hospital."

"What's happened? Are you alright?"

What she says next stumps me completely. "I've been blown up in town."

***

She means it too. Find her at Lincoln County Hospital. In a cubicle in A&E. Looking very much the worse for wear. A stitched cut across her forehead and a bandaged arm. There's a police officer sitting on a chair waiting to talk to her. Explain who I am and she lets me go in to see Alicia. A young Asian doctor checking her sight. Holding each eyelid open in turn and shining a narrow-beamed torch onto the pupil. Alicia nods to me in recognition. And smiles. Wanly. As soon as Doctor Rahman's done, she puts her arms out for a hug. Hold her tightly awaiting enlightenment. She doesn't say anything.

"Well? You've been in the wars then."

"Uh-huh."

"What on earth have you been doing?"

"Nothing. I got up soon after you left. Walked into work. It was still early and I fancied a bacon buttie but I hadn't got enough money on me. So I came down Guildhall Street. I was walking up to the bank when the cashpoint... Well I don't know what happened. It just exploded!"

Both of us shaking our heads now. Keep hugging. Long minutes until the policewoman puts her head round the curtains. "The doc says it's okay to interview you. Can we talk now?"

"I suppose so."

She pulls out a notebook and asks Alicia about timings and where she was exactly when it all went off and whether she saw anybody near the bank. She says not. Can't help much at all.

"Okay then." Resignedly closes the notebook and puts the pen away in its clip.

She's let me sit in on her brief interview but has volunteered nothing from which we might better understand anything at all. So I ask the obvious. "What just happened to Alicia?"

"As far as we can tell it was an attempt to rob the cash machine. They opened the flap, fed in a length of hose, squirted in a bottleful of camper gas. And set it off."

"How?"

"Dunno yet. A fuse of some sort. Or they say it's now possible to do it with sound-waves from a special sort of mobile phone they're making in Romania. They didn't get anything 'cause the machine's got great pins going down into the concrete underneath and the inside's one of the new ones like a hard plastic shell which folds in on itself when there's a fire or something like this. No money came out. But the blast blew stonework off the bank clear across the street. And a woman opening up the tobacconists shop is dead. Killed outright. So now it's murder. You were a very lucky young lady." The officer's no more than a year or two older than Alicia but just at that moment she looks decades more haggard than my darling girl, despite all of Alicia's cuts and bruises. Shakes her head to clear it of troubling thoughts. "I have to go. If there's anything else you remember when you can think about it, phone us or come in and see me. Will you do that, please?"

"Of course I will."

Alicia won't let go of me and it's quite some time before I can get her discharged to come home in the car with me.

Open the door and let her go in ahead of me. As Alicia bends to pick up the sparse pile of post beneath the letterbox, catch a glimpse of a business card among the white envelopes before she screws it up. The only two words on it I can make out are the phrase *Financial arrangement*. Going to ask her who it's from but she's already heading for the kitchen. Persuade her to let me make the tea and get her settled comfortably on the settee. Totally effective distraction.

Lincoln's on the national as well as the local television news come the evening bulletins. Graphic images of that end of Guildhall Street looking like a war zone. Police tapes. Piles of rubble. Broken windows. An excited reporter in the foreground with very little by way of hard facts to pad out his two minutes. He doesn't tell us anything we don't already know.

The post only comes back into my mind once Alicia's in bed asleep and I'm tidying up. Look in the waste paper basket and the kitchen bin but can't find the crumpled card.

***

Alicia doesn't want to stay home on her own. Insists on walking in to City Hall with me next day. High on painkillers and showing a contrasting mix of obstinacy and vulnerability.

The week drags on. They're hunting for an Eastern European gang. Probably Czech. Long gone of course. It's happened a few times on the continent. Mainly in Holland and Germany. Not so much here.

Resolve to take Alicia away for the weekend. Into the countryside. Somewhere quiet and calm. To my surprise she doesn't want that. She seems to have tapped into a wellspring of nervous energy. "I want to work on the new house. Get it done." We demolish an internal wall to create a single living room from the separate dining room and lounge. Swinging sledgehammers in turns and clearing away the block-work and chunks of old plaster into a skip outside. Drink a beer or two. And finally, in exhaustion, sleep for eight hours solid. Rising early on Sunday to do an eleven mile trudge in the Peak District with Steve, Alex and Saul. First really hard training for the Three Peaks Challenge. Ensuring another good night's sleep.

***

In the office another week and they're still talking about the bank raid. The debris has been cleared from the vicinity of the Guildhall and all the window glass having been replaced there's no reason not to hold the regular meeting of full council in its normal venue. Don't rush to get there early. If I get there before the meeting starts I'll only be spending time telling any councillors I've not seen in the office recently what happened to Alicia. And I'm tired of repeating myself. She was incredibly lucky to walk away with a few abrasions and cuts and a bad headache. End of story. Unless she remembers something to advance the criminal investigation. She hasn't and can't. And the council meeting itself? Business-like. Boring. And over-long. Instilling a deep-rooted desire to be home on my settee with Alicia and a large, hot cup of tea. Get there eventually but not soon enough.

***

The rest of February is simply strange. By which I mean inexplicably devoid of interest or novelty. And rendered problematic by Alicia's mood-swings. Up and down. Lurching between phases of extrovert energy and withdrawal. Not much sharing or discussion going on. Although considerable progress is being made in finishing Alicia's latest house refurbishment. Professionals are doing the tiling and putting in the new kitchen and we're painting anything that stands still long enough.

I'd quite thought we'd be talking about future skiing after getting all that gear and trying Andorra. Maybe planning to take lessons at the Snowdome over in Staffordshire or its equivalent in Milton Keynes. And then booking another winter holiday for next year. But something happens to turn Alicia completely off the notion. News of her friend Julie. Now Jools is an excellent and highly experienced skier but the word is that she's likely to be in hospital for months after hitting a tree or a rock or something.

And who knows what long-term damage she'll carry from that. Guess we'll go and see her as soon as they fly her back to an English hospital. So skiing becomes an unwelcome subject for discussion and all our gear, used only once, goes into a suitcase in my roofspace.

The final proof for me that Alicia's struggling with coming to terms with her near-brush with death as well as with Julie's misfortune is the one thing she doesn't do. She doesn't go looking to find a new coat to replace the one slashed by flying slivers of brick and glass from the bank.

The only thing to be grateful for. No more worrying or problematic post for Alicia. Unless she's coming back to my house at lunchtime to snaffle and hide it. Don't like the fact I'm thinking this way. It's about trust. Put it out of my head. Just hope the email traffic from Darryl is thinning out too.

What does come through the letterbox, along with unwanted bills and boring circulars, are a couple of truly wonderful communications. The first, in a beautifully-lettered, white envelope, is a wedding invitation. Plus guest. From an old colleague whose daughter is taking the plunge. So I've reached the stage when the next generation's old enough not only to vote but to settle down. A strange feeling. Mind you late spring in Cambridgeshire sounds an appealing prospect. A chance to show Alicia off. Get her a new dress. Doubtless that means new shoes as well. Put the date on the calendar. Hoping by then Alicia's back in the right frame of mind to enjoy it.

The other piece of personal post that's out of the ordinary and even better than the wedding invitation comes from the Watford County Court. It's a certificate. An expensively-won Decree Nisi. A good night to celebrate. Take Alicia out to the Italian. Only to bump into Clare and Patrick and it's Alicia who readily agrees the notion of sharing a table for four. I'd have kept her to myself. When Patrick makes us tell him why we're out on the town he insists on ordering a bottle of champagne. And Alicia suggests a second one before we're too deep into our main courses. Dessert wine with coffee ensures the need for a taxi home in preference to the staggering lope which would otherwise have had to pass for walking.

***

Time to see the dentist. The check-up reveals no fillings necessary. So a de-scale and polish for my teeth, lying back in the elevated recumbent position peculiar to surgical chairs. My dentist, Gina, isn't one of those who insists on conversing with you when your mouth's full of metal tools so I come close to relaxing. Eyes closed, thumbs hooked into trouser pockets and fingers lying across my belly, brain elsewhere, thinking about Alicia. Not that I reach any conclusions. Other than the obvious ones; I've got pretty strong feelings for her, sex with her is wonderful and I understand her not at all.

"That's done."

"Thank you."

Now she wants to talk. Asking about work and holiday plans. There must be a gap in her timetable before the next patient. We touch on skiing. Agree that the exercise and high mountain air is good for us. Concur that Andorra is excellent value for money compared to Eurozone resorts. And part friends. Albeit that one us carries a lightened wallet.

Have you ever considered just how much time you spend sitting in a chair being tended to in our service-oriented economy? At the hairdresser and the dentist for starters. Worse if you're a girl. Getting your nails done. Or a pedicure. Or, an increasingly popular one lately, the tattooist. Not sure how that became as prevalent a habit as it has. After all, despite everything immigration has thrown our way, we still live in a society rooted in Judaeo-Christian tradition and one of its ancient tenets was that marking your skin was a sin. It's why the tattooed numbers inflicted at Auschwitz, Dachau and Ravensbruck were such an insult to the faith of their recipients.

Don't think I'd want a tattoo anyway but Alicia already has one. A tiny swallow in flight, delicately inked above her left shoulder blade. Ask her why she has it and she won't tell me. Other than "I felt like it." Which is okay, I guess. Huddled up to her back as she sleeps, let my fingers softly trace its outlines. And wonder about her idiosyncrasies and contradictions. She's body conscious but

120

she eats like a horse. So much of her life is dedicated to earning cold cash but she spends it as fast as she makes it. She seems strangely distanced much of the time from her cousin and the people she calls friends but says she likes being close to me. So she acts as though I'm important to her but has never once said she loves me. There's a veil over all her emotions disguising the direction she wants her life to take and her motivations. Even though I think I know her better than anybody, she's still an enigma I need to but can't fathom. Without spooking her. This is a woman who'll disappear if challenged.

Plenty of time to think. And with the Three Peaks Challenge looming ever closer there's plenty to think about. I'm a member of a gym over at Burton Waters and take advice from my allocated fitness assessor, a very young but extremely confident man called Ollie. He suggests doing four or five miles walking each day to build up stamina. And upping it to six to twelve miles at weekends. "Distance is more important than doing inclines at this point."

Get a pedometer and find it's not so very hard to fit in that sort of mileage around my current workload. Weekdays I can walk to the gym and back or I can get up early and go out over the common or up and down Steep Hill taking in circuits of the cathedral.

On Saturday or Sunday, when I can inveigle Alicia away from her building project, we take the car and go further afield. Onto the Lincolnshire Wolds. Up to Beverley and beyond into Yorkshire proper. As far as Flamborough Head, Robin Hood's Bay, Whitby and Ilkley. The northern uplands and moors are starkly beautiful. If cold and wet this time of year.

If it's sometimes hard to keep going, there are fringe benefits. Lose nearly a stone of flab and gain vastly more energy for both work and the horizontal aspects of life. Still love the job but am developing a definite preference for the latter.

***

Days come and go when I'm under the illusion I've cracked it. That I'm in control of what's going on. That I'm making everything move in the direction I need it to go. But if that's vaguely the case for work, it's completely untrue of my personal life. Alicia blows hot and cold. Leaving me exasperated when she chooses to absent herself and to exclude me from her burgeoning property business. Or ecstatic when she's in a loving mood and stays over. The trouble is it's hard to predict where we'll be on any given day or to plan anything longer term.

Eventually the solution becomes to go ahead and do whatever I want, giving her the choice to join in but ploughing on regardless when she doesn't or can't. If the day job required the sort of long hours I was used to in London, I'd mind less. But I hate being on my own. No good at it. Never was a reader. Nor particularly a boozer. So burying my head in a book or occupying a stool in The Queen in the West aren't really options. The only beneficiary is my physical health because long sessions at the gym become the norm. I don't have to think when I'm driving myself to exhaustion on the machines or lifting stupid stacks of weights. Do feel better on the training walks for Three Peaks. Keep up with Saul much more easily. Although still getting occasional breathing difficulties. Need to shift my registration to a local doctor and get checked out. If it's asthmatic in origin they should be able to give me an inhaler or something.

Keep stepping up my fitness regime. Train harder. The walking is good but it's pretty flat round here apart from Steep Hill over and doing that over and over again gets boring. And being in the gym after work isn't enough. Running could help but trying it again in Dubai unequivocally proved to me that my knees won't take it anymore. Talk it over as part of a general health check with my new doctor. He suggests biking. "Good exercise. Your back's supported and it's low impact on your joints. Try it by all means."

Alicia seizes on the idea gleefully. "Could fancy that. Get ourselves matching bikes. Hybrids are good. More comfortable than pure road bikes or off-road machines. Still light though and good gears." How does she know this stuff? "Can't see us on old sit-up-and-begs." Don't let her go mad though. Five hundred apiece buys us Ridgebacks. Mine blue. Hers hot pink. Both pretty much the same size given her long legs.

Lincolnshire's lack of gradients means soon enough we're doing fair distances with only an occasional need to resort to lower gearing for the slight rises which pass for hills in the countryside around here. Trip mileage increases each week until we're visiting large chunks of the county at the weekend. Much easier to do it in Alicia's company and fortunately it seems what's left to do on her latest residential project can safely be left to the builders. With luck she'll have it on the rental market by April and we can start banking an income against the mortgage payments. Or it'll be sold to fund the next.

Cycling causes more weight to drop off slowly but surely. Off-setting buffet lunches and council dinners. Feeling better and better. As for the walking, we're done with Yorkshire and The Peak District. Ready to start more practise on the real thing. We may not be able to travel up to Ben Nevis before the day but there's no reason not to do Scafell Pike and Snowdon again before we have to climb all of them on the same day.

Enlist Jane's advice in the wretched matter of getting sponsorship. We may be doing the Three Peaks Challenge primarily to stretch ourselves but the team want to raise a bit for good charitable causes on the back of the physical effort. Jane understands without my saying a word that as the boss I feel a bit embarrassed tapping up my staff for cash but tells me not to be daft. "We'll have posters on the office door and at reception. I'll keep pledge forms for people to sign and I'm happy to chase up payments after the event. You don't want to be doing that." She says it as a fact. She's right.

"Thank you so much. Don't know what I'd do without you."

"Well I could stand a pay rise." She laughs. Flounces out with attitude before I can reply.

***

Already it's a year since my first council elections. A fallow year for the city council this time around. But I'm still Deputy Returning Officer for the Lincoln wards of the county council. Not the same personal stake in the results. And City Hall doesn't virtually close down like last year because many of the staff working on the election aren't my employees. The turnout's the lowest I've ever seen and it's hardly the most arduous of duties. The cheque at the end's worth banking though. Don't tell Alicia how much. She'll only come up with plans to spend it. Whereas I'll do the sensible thing and pay another chunk off my mortgage.

On Friday I knock off and go home early. Feel I've earned it. Get there to find a big man waiting on the doorstep. Wearing a tight-fitting blue suit. And scowling. Know him immediately for what he is but glance down at his feet anyway. Times have changed. He's wearing Doc Martins. My Dad used to say you could always tell a bailiff by his footwear. The standing instruction in our family was *If it's a man with brown boots, Dad's not in.* Never very good with money, my Dad. It came and went, seldom at the same time as the debt collectors. And we moved a lot when I was a boy.

"Yes?"

A man of few words, he says "Good afternoon" and hands me a card. It carries the name of a firm of court certified bailiffs and his personal details. He then states his business in short order. "Miss Alicia Valency."

Two potential responses spring to mind. Either *You don't look anything like her.* Or *No, I'm not her.* But suspect he's the type to lack a sense of humour. Try the polite approach. "What can I do for you?"

"Warning before County Court action to serve, sir. Will you sign for it please?"

Suppose I could refuse but, beyond delaying things a little, what would that achieve? Sign where requested and go in, weighing the manila envelope in my hand.

Now of course I want to know what's inside. But I can't open it. This is Alicia's business not mine. Put it on the kitchen table. Can't stay here looking at it though. Need thinking space. Going back into the office is no good. After hours there's always a steady flow of people dropping in to see me on the off-chance. Head for the cinema. God knows what I watch. Simply take a ticket for the next available showing. Buy a chocolate muffin and a cardboard cup of coffee. The container is cardboard I mean. Not the drink. Head for the back of the auditorium and take cautious sips of my steaming coffee until the house lights go down and the adverts start to roll. Then my mind empties and settles and my sub-conscious goes to work on the problems of the hour.

It's always been this way as long as I can remember. The cinema is where I relax most completely. I'll watch any film that's on and feel better at the end of it. It doesn't matter to me if I'm one of a mass audience or on my own. I'm entirely comfortable being the only person in the place. My friends think that's weird but they didn't have my turbulent upbringing.

After my Dad died, my Mum made ends meet by taking a job at the local cinema. They weren't all owned by chains back then and this one was independent. The guy owned another one in the next town but that was it. Just the two. Anyway Mum started as a ticket seller. Inherited the book-keeping for the business. Made such a decent fist of it that after six months the owner made her the manager. From then on I spent most of the hours there when I wasn't in school. My sisters and I worked there evenings, weekends and holidays, ushering, selling pop-corn, chocolates, ice-creams and orangeade and clearing away the detritus left on the seats and floor at the end of each performance. If the weather or the current film left the cinema empty, as occasionally happened, the three of us would sit there and get Sid, the projectionist, to screen whatever he had in his stock of cans of film. Just for us.

Sometimes Mum would join us which was a real treat. To hear her laugh or sing along or shed tears with us as the giant figures on the screen told us their stories. Usually she'd be too busy with paperwork or helping out the cleaner, who suffered from something called lumbago. I've never known what that was.

So cinema is in my blood. It's where I come to brood, to think, to reach out for inspiration and to decide what to do next. Or in this case to work out what's wrong with Alicia and how to help her sort it out.

I know we're talking debts and overspending. Of course we are. But why does she buy so much stuff she doesn't need and can't afford? Does it compensate for something missing in her life? Lack of love? I love her to bits so why's that not enough? Plainly it isn't.

There's a phrase in common usage. Consume your own smoke. Emotionally speaking I think it means that you can't change how another person acts towards or feels about you and confronting them will only make them feel worse and mean they're likely to blame you because they associate you with the negative kickback. But what you can deal with is your own instinctive reaction to them and your feelings about how they are. You can just accept them as they happen to be. Help by all means. But never judge. Reward change. Accentuate the positive as the song has it. Just do nothing that can be perceived as an attack. Difficult. Yes indeed. But the essential approach.

So no criticism when I come in to find Alicia cooking pasta. Just an offer of help. "What was the hand-delivered letter today? Anything I can help you with?"

"No. Just a bit of cash-flow on the works. It'll be fine when I get to sell out."

Take that at face value or not? Question her further? No way.

***

My working days settle back down into an acceptable pattern. Interesting tasks appropriately offset by repetitive matters requiring only charm and the application of common sense. But I'm becoming seriously concerned about Alicia. She's working too many hours after she finishes at the office. There's a weariness in her. Sometimes she lays her head against my shoulder, looks up at me and I can see it in her eyes. Sheer exhaustion.

And I'm tired too. Physically. And a little shorter-tempered.

Sundays are now dedicated to serious team sprints up and down bits of the English landscape. Sometimes Alicia and Jess come along. Other times Alicia cries off pleading the need to work on her latest house project. As it nears completion, she begins negotiating to buy another one. I remind her the plan had been to get stuck in to doing up my house once she finished her three storey townhouse and suggest we make a proper start on it last.

"No. We don't want mess all round us. Do we? This is okay for now. While I sort out the next one."

"The next one?"

"I've got a bid in for another one round the corner."

"Oh yeah."

"What?"

"Nothing." Inside I'm seething. Patrick was right to warn me all those weeks ago. She's pulled a fait accompli. Handed me a done deal. On a bad day like this it feels like I'm running a way station or a useful hotel while her own surroundings are in turmoil. Not fair. Not going to tolerate it. Got to have this out with her.

Just not today.

***

The team manages to climb Scafell Pike on a fine mid-May afternoon. A repeat climb up Snowdon the following weekend proves more difficult because of the weather. Snow on the top and fog closing in as we near the summit. In deference to common-sense, we give that up as a bad job. No point in being stupid and risking our lives on an exercise. It'll be easier come next month we tell ourselves.

Get in late evening. Alicia's in front of the television. An empty wine bottle and used glass on the coffee table in front of her.

"Where've you been?" Immediately abrasive.

"Road works. Bad traffic. Snowdonia's a long way."

"You could've phoned."

"I tried. You didn't answer. And I texted you."

She picks up her mobile from the coffee table. Puts it down again listlessly. "No battery." She starts to cry. "I wanted you."

Gets angry when I try to take her into my arms." You can go to hell. I don't even like you." It doesn't get much better from there either.

Sorrowful as hell next morning. "I'm sorry. Whoever that was yesterday, it wasn't me."

"Not you? So you're not taking any responsibility then? Who was it, if it wasn't you?"

"No. I mean it wasn't a part of me I'm very proud of. I shouldn't have drunk so much. And I shouldn't have taken it out on you. That's what I'm sorry about."

"Okay."

"Are we cool then?"

"Yes we are. Frosty. But we need to talk about what's getting to you. You seem under a lot of pressure. It's not still Darryl hassling you is it?"

"No it isn't. And he's not going to get to us again."

"Don't promise what you might not be able to deliver. But alright. Are you going to tell me what's going on? With you."

"I'm sorting it out. It's just money. The financing."

"That's all?"

"Isn't that enough?"

"It's not about us then?"

"No. God no!"

Nodding. Letting it go. Once again. For now.

***

The others are out doing serious training at the end of May with three weeks to go to the real thing but I can't. I've got an enforced break. A wedding to go to. With Alicia.

The marriage is being celebrated in one of those idyllic Cambridgeshire villages in which the essential spirit of England has somehow prevailed over the depredations of modern house-builders. It's got a picturesque church with a square tower and a walled graveyard. And a village green. Today with a large marquee on it. It probably helps that if you want to come here you drive into the village, do whatever you came to do and drive out the way you came in. No through traffic. A great bonus in the battle for preservation of the old ways of living.

The bride is leaving from her family home, a couple of hundred yards from the church and the guests can park nearby and stroll up casually and safely. God's smiling down on us or her and it's a gloriously sunny day.

The church is awash with flowers and the service full of the traditionally lovely moments. And at every single one of them I find myself exchanging glances and broad smiles with Alicia. Afterwards the photographer, as they always seem to, takes his time over the family photographs. No second chances If he screws up there are no second chancesI suppose so he might as well take just one more and then yet another one for posterity. Leave him to it. Sit on the bench in the shade of the porch looking across at the children running over the graves. With an arm round Alicia's waist. She leans in to me. Sighs.

After a moment or so she says "Weddings make you think. Don't they?"

"Yeah they do. What's on your mind?"

"What the future holds for us. Whether I'll ever get married again."

"Don't you want to?"

"Not after the disaster I made of it last time around."

"My view exactly. Just got divorced. Why would I want to go through that again?" And immediately wish I could snatch my words back. The anguished look on her face. Hurt and sorrow in equal measure, swiftly controlled by an immense effort of will. I'm not supposed to have agreed with her.

"I'll feel differently in a few months, I'm sure." The best I can do in the circumstances.

She avoids taking my hand as we walk out of the church gate and back onto the green.

It wouldn't be fair to accuse Alicia of sulking. She comes round far quicker than I suspect I would in her shoes. And she joins in with all the fun. Chats eagerly to all the strangers on our table. Learns their life stories and ensures neither of us is left out of anything. Laughs in all the right places during the speeches. Plays with the little ones. Eats whatever's put in front of her. Drinks sparingly. But throughout it all she carries herself as though slightly removed from the whole thing. An observer rather than a full-blooded participant. Only when darkness falls and the marquee lights are dimmed for the band to start in on their repertoire of slower tunes does she relax and allow me to lead her by the hand into the floor. To come into my arms and hold on tightly. A flashback. Not immediately sure where from. But then it comes to me. It's the elderly couple in Istanbul. For fleeting moments dancing with Alicia, I feel like they must have. Smiling broadly. Alicia notices and starts to comment but I'm not having any. "Shush you. Enjoy the moment."

She does. And we do.

***

The following weekend we take our lives in our hands and cycle over the Dunham bridge into Nottinghamshire with cars whizzing past us on the twisting approach roads. Find a cafe for a belated but very full English breakfast. Come home sluggishly. But safely.

Absurdly two days later at Nettleham, Police Headquarters of all places, I get myself into a little accident.

***

My turn to be sitting on the couch in a curtained off booth in Accident and Emergency. Where Clare finds me.

"What the hell happened to you?"

"I got lucky."

"You're still here so suppose you are. What was it?"

"Someone nearly put a shell from a Heckler and Koch in me."

"You probably deserved it. Seriously, what happened?"

"A real cock-up. She could've killed all three of us if the instructor hadn't grabbed the gun off her."

"Three of you?"

"Her husband, the Mayor, Tony Everett and me."

"No shit!" Everett's the Chief Constable. Trouble incarnate in a situation like this. "How on earth could that happen?"

"Horrifyingly easily."

"You were up at Nettleham?"

"Yep. Doing the tour. Messing about on the skid pans, inspecting the dogs, lunch with the Chief and then a go on the firing range."

Clare grimaces. "Heads'll roll. This stuff is supposed to be closely supervised."

"The instructions were clear enough. Point and shoot down range. One at a time. Taking turns so only one gun out. With an instructor standing right beside us. Maintain position and let the instructor take the gun back and make safe. We let the mayoress go first and God knows what she was doing. She must have thought the magazine was empty so she turns and her finger's still on the trigger. Miracle she didn't kill us all before he grabbed her. Anyway she put four rounds in the ceiling. "

"Bloody hell."

"Pretty extreme approach to handling marital dischord with her husband."

Clare laughs. Venting relief. "Cheaper than a divorce. But if you weren't hit, why are you here?"

"Fractured a rib hitting the floor."

"Does Alicia know where you are?"

Shake my head. "She doesn't know what's happened. I better ring her. Will in a bit. Didn't want to alarm her."

"Don't leave it too long."

"Hey. You know what was really funny? The speed at which the mayor and the chief and me dived off our chairs."

"Sheer adrenalin."

"Apart from that I'm okay really. Glad to be here still."

She gives me a piercingly perceptive look then. The one good police officers use sparingly and well. Letting you know they're on to you. "No you're not alright. What else?"

"Nothing really. Just struggling a bit. And there's no real reason for it. Things are much better with Alicia. She says she's sorted out her money issues. We're getting along really well. Life should be good. And yet I feel really down."

"It's a reaction. And it's perfectly natural. Why do you think teachers always get sick at the beginning of the holidays?"

"I never really thought about it."

"Because being a rock for people you care about when they're in trouble takes everything you have. And when you stop having to play that role you've nothing left to fight with. Whether it's a cold or a dodgy curry or the slightest emotional upset. Or even being shot at. You're going to fall over. That's the way it is. So don't beat yourself up. It'll pass."

"Not sure the Chief Constable will see it that way."

"Ah. That's a whole different issue."

***

They let me take a taxi home. Eventually. With a dressing strapped around my rib cage. Underneath a torn shirt. Extremely uncomfortable.

Alicia's not there. And I still can't raise her on the phone. Change and limp painfully round to her house. Nobody answering the doorbell. The hue of the day shifts into still darker shades of grey with my mood. She doesn't come back. And I won't try to phone her again. Being obstinate. Probably cutting off my own nose to spite my face.

Don't even try to contact her at work next day. Really angry with her. And it doesn't help that my freshly re-bandaged side is seriously painful. And at home that night she walks in perfectly normally. As though nothing untoward's happened. Perhaps for her it hasn't. Can't help myself. Should just trust her but have to ask. "Where were you last night?"

Her answer's off-hand. "Working late. Planning for the next renovation." Gives me a sharp look. "You're not starting to go all possessive on me are you?"

Only one possible answer to that. "No of course not. I just wondered if it's unreasonable to expect to have you around when you've just been shot at."

Not quite true but worth it for the shock on her face.

CHAPTER X: MID-JUNE

The forward planning pays off right from the start. Especially saving ourselves from having to drive to Scotland and then start the challenge as soon as we get there. So up to the Highlands on Friday afternoon. Getting past the worst of the painfully slow M6 snarl-ups before rush hour traffic turns them into complete nightmares. Early tea around The Lake District. Change of driver. Matt re-taking the wheel from Saul. Push on. Slow through Glasgow and onto rural Scottish roads heading for the Highlands. Running along beside Loch Lomond. Up to Crianlarich. And beyond.

I could give you a load of guff about how beautiful the scenery is. But I'm paying it not one jot of attention. All I'm worried about, considering the terrain, is just how tough the climbing's going to be and how much my side is going to trouble me.

We could have headed straight for Fort William to stay there overnight. But Matt and I are in cahoots. Both with a love of history. Rather than let the gang just potter aimlessly about on Saturday morning, we're going to be staying north of Oban with a diversionary plan. Find our B&B. Dump our bags. Nosh and beer in a pub. Not too much of the latter. Nor too early a night. Excitement and nerves are hardly great precursors of sound sleep. Alex's snores keep me from dropping off awhile anyway but eventually drift off as well.

Wake early. The day presenting itself behind the curtains is grey and industrial. Promising only cold and windy summits to climb. Alex still in bed and still lightly snoring. Head down to breakfast on my own, the quiet bustle of the landlady adding to the grim tension I'm already feeling. Bacon, eggs and a square of processed pink sausage-meat settle things down a little.

On my third cup of tea and able to smile when joined by the others. Arriving together, chatting and laughing. Trying to convince themselves we're neither madly over-ambitious nor plain stupid to be doing this. To be trying to complete over twenty-five ascending and descending miles within the time limit, without seizing up or getting bogged down in traffic on the roads between the three mountains we've set ourselves to conquer. The real thing vastly different to any of our training hikes. Knowing there's no go-slow option and yet we have to exercise care because the whole team can be disabled by a crippling accident to any one of us. Wanting to get started on the first peak right now but knowing we have to stick to the plan and wait the day out, conserving our energy and consuming the good meals we'll need inside us to fuel a twenty-four hour marathon. Pull myself together. We're not going to spend the day fretting about getting up Ben Nevis, the one mountain which is completely unfamiliar to us. Instead we're going to take a shortish drive. First to Appin and then to Ballachulish. Plenty of time to get over to Fort William and the challenge afterwards.

***

Get Matt to stop so I can check the map. Nearly there. Off onto a little forestry road. "We walk from here." Moans and groans but everybody climbs out onto the rough track stretching uphill. Not too steep.

Saul adds his warning as team leader. "Watch your ankles. Be a shame to crash out before we even start." He's right of course. Taking care definitely the order of the day.

Up into the forest. Through an initially dense palisade of tall firs, following a poorly defined footpath. As well I've been here before. Although many years ago when it looked very different. The trees were much shorter then, allowing more light onto the forest floor. For a moment thinking brings doubt that I'm in the right place but then spot the monument just ahead. "There it is."

"Is that all we're here for? What is it?"

The team gathers round it to read the plaque on the little cairn but it doesn't mean much without the explanation I'm only to happy to provide.

"Did you ever read *Kidnapped* by Robert Louis Stevenson when you were kids?" A nod or two. "Or see the appalling film with Michael Caine. Not one of his finer moments." More

135

acknowledgements. "In the story young Davy Balfour witnesses a murder. Stevenson didn't make that up. The murder really happened. Right here. Only it wasn't a cultivated forest then. It was a natural glen but with plenty of trees and rocks for cover. The King's factor, his land agent in these parts was a man named Colin Campbell of Glenure. He wasn't actually that unpopular even though this is only six years after Culloden. But this man's a Campbell and his allegiance is to London. Not to the King over the Water like the Stewart clan who live round here. They're Jacobites. And he's a tax collector. Don't suppose he ever went that easy on them. As he's riding up here, he can be recognised at some distance. Not just from the richness of his coat but because he's not wearing a wig and he's got a shock of bright copper-coloured hair. The colour of Alicia's. Behind his back, they call him The Red Fox. So Colin Campbell's riding along here and he's shot on this very spot by a man lurking in cover behind some trees in a heavy brown coat and carrying a long old musket. The Red Fox falls off his horse, dying in the arms of his kinsman Mungo Campbell. It's a pretty bleak place to die. And a hard death. Kicking at the pain of a musket ball in the back."

Pause for dramatic effect and to make sure they're all still with me. They are.

"In the story as Stevenson wrote it, Davy chases after the man in the coat with the gun. Loses sight of him among the trees but runs into Alan Breck, the companion in his own adventures. Alan swears blind he didn't shoot the Red Fox and Davy doesn't know if he can believe him."

"And..." Saul, speaking for them all.

"So you want to know how it panned out?"

"Bloody hell! Course we do. Come on. Out with it."

Everybody loves a story. Keep them hanging on a second or two longer. In anticipation. "These are the lands of the Stewart clan. The laird's a man known as James of the Glens. And he isn't giving any of his clan up to the English. Even if he doesn't know who did it for sure, nothing much moves without his say-so and he must suspect who the culprit is. And the King's officers know it.

So they arrest James and imprison him in a Campbell stronghold. Inverary Castle. But he still won't talk."

"Is that it?"

"No. Back to the car. Something else to look at."

Direct Matt until we reach the Ballachulish Bridge. "Before we get out let me tell you this. When they tried James Stewart as an accessory to the murder of Colin Campbell of Glenure, there were eleven Campbells on the jury. So he didn't exactly get a fair trial. Come on. Let me show you."

Another monument. another plaque. *Erected 1911 To the memory of James Stewart of Acharn James of the Glens. Executed on this spot Nov.8th 1757 for a crime of which he was not guilty.*

"The soldiers brought him back here into Stewart lands to hang him. As a deterrent to his clansmen. They let the body rot here in chains until it stank to high heaven and had to be buried. No last minute reprieve for James Stewart. Anyway legend has it that the secret of who slew the Red Fox is handed down from father to son among the clan leadership to this very day. And it's still a secret. They wouldn't tell Stevenson which is why in *Kidnapped* it's an unsolved murder mystery. In the book as in real life. Is that a good yarn or what?"

Several voices murmuring approval. But one cuts through all the others. Alex's. "Can we go and get a drink now?"

***

One beer apiece in the pub with our lunch. Rationing imposed by Saul definitely a wise move. Before we drive up to the foot of Ben Nevis. It's getting cooler still as the afternoon wears on which is probably good as long as the temperature doesn't drop too far down.

First scare isn't on the mountain. It's in the car-park of the Ben Nevis Inn at Achentee at three-thirty in the afternoon. A very full car-park without any space to dump our car. "Bloody hell. Plan B time already" says Matt, swinging the car round to block the exit. "Let's get the gear out and I'll drive down to the visitor centre and

137

park up there. I don't think that's very far from here. I'll drive back over in three or four hours so I'll be here when you get off the mountain. Get me on the mobile if you need me to do anything before that. If any of you can get a signal. Okay?"

Saul agrees so we jump out and start hauling out our gear. Our fleeces and waterproofs and the lightweight day-packs containing the camelback drink bladders we filled up this morning with Saul's patent isotonic mixture. Apple and mango juice diluted with water and a little salt, a remedy for cramp. Pull on my rain-resistant over-trousers. Saul doles out emergency sandwiches to carry with us. Alex stuffs his straight into his grinning gob. "Less to carry." Get the rest of our stuff out. Hand out the walking poles. Everybody gets their boots on. Check my pack's contents for the umpteenth time. The sarnies, jelly babies, the best source of instant sugar for the blood stream ever devised by man, extra bootlaces, the spare map and compass safe alongside the packs of nuts, raisins and chocolate and a woolly hat for later. All present and correct.

The time ticks slowly away. Another look at my wristwatch. Two minutes to four. Eager to set off now. Watching the seconds tick by. Finally it's four o'clock. Sixteen hundred hours. "Zero hour" says Saul. His prerogative as team leader. High fives all round. Time to go. "Let's do this." Twenty-four hours of hell starts here and now. "Have a good one, guys."

Going to need it. The air feels cooler still now, any residual warmth from the day seeping away, almost gone.

And we take the first steps. Alongside a couple of other teams. Some guys in red charity t-shirts. Another group who are obviously soldiers or marines. Hard, fit men carrying big khaki packs on their backs. And there's a third gang too; of young men and women with no discernible common approach when it comes to colour or functionality of clothing or equipment. They make our quartet look highly organised by comparison. All keen though. Jockeying to be first through the pub gate. Hear one of the girls ask "Which one's Ben Nevis?" She gets a gruff response from one of her companions. "The big one over there." His vague wave of the arm compounds a lie. You can't see the mountain at all from here. I've spent ages looking at the map. It's hidden off to the left.

A strangely ordinary way to start the challenge. Up the hillside. Over the low crest of the first ridge. A stile to be negotiated. Already worried. Finding it hard to catch my breath. It's not my ribs either. Afraid it's the asthma which hasn't really troubled me in years. Swallowing then coughing. Conscious attempts to relax and breathe properly through my nose. Hard to do. Need to pull more air in and that means a mouth gasping with effort. Root around in my pocket for the blue and brown inhalers. Stop and take a hit of each. Seems to help a bit. The others already several yards ahead of me. Must keep up. Increase my pace up the zig-zagging track. The only positive for me remains that the ache in my side is hardly troubling me at all.

It's not too bad underfoot. Cleared ground paved with vast slabs of rough stone. And the incline isn't very steep. Find I'm calmer. This is easy compared to what's coming later. Plod on by a metal footbridge across a stream. Then another similar bridge. Straightening up. Trying to move a bit faster. Not to be left behind. And, as suddenly as it arrived, my breathing difficulty passes. I've got my second wind and feel okay. Have the energy to look around as we pass a small cluster of casual walkers coming down the mountain without any proper gear. Trainers and carrier bags as though they're traipsing up the main street through Fort William. Presumably not trying to do the Three Peaks Challenge. But who knows? If they were I'd be envious they're nearly down off Ben Nevis and we've a good five hours to go to be able to say that.

Up ahead Alex stops walking and looks back. Waits for me to reach him. "You alright?"

Nod. Saving my breath. Pass him and close in on Saul and Steve. The two of them are grinning and chattering away like the day-trippers we've just passed back there.

Veering left. Even though the soldier-boys are far out of sight already, I'm adopting military strategy. Empty my mind and keep my eyes on the feet of the man in front. Supposedly the miles then pass with reduced consciousness and suffering. Fat chance. Wish it was Alicia's arse in my line of vision.

Unhelpful to think about Alicia. Her not answering her phone today and me desperate to speak to her. To have heard her voice wishing me luck. But not even a text from her. Shit. Must get her out of my head. Can't fret about her now. Keep walking. Stop thinking. About anything and everything except how thirsty I feel. Pull the mouthpiece out and taste my fruit juice mixture. Roll it round my mouth. Swallow and moisten my lips with my tongue. Another sip or two. The others have stopped to put on their fleeces and waterproof tops. It's definitely colder. Follow suit and put my hat on too. And carry on. Zigzagging left and right up the path. Rising steadily up the side of the valley.

Steve stops for a brief consultation with the map. "Just ahead. That must be Lachan Meall an t-Suidhe."

"Which means...?"

"The half-way lachan."

"And what the hell's a lachan?"

"No idea. But if it's halfway, let's have five minute's rest."

Break out the chocolate and Saul produces some mint-cake. Pure sugar. Wonderful stuff. Tooth-decaying but hugely reviving.

"What do you call a woman whose son's got an Oedipus Complex?"

"Dunno. What would you call her?"

"A Milf."

Worth a hint of a laugh. Halfway up a mountain.

"You can thank Lee Mack for that one. What do you call a man who can't stand North Face jackets?"

"Go on."

"Anoraknophobic."

Groan.

Time for a push from Saul. Looks pointedly at his watch. "Come on. Break over. Gotta get on." The five minutes over far too soon. Into motion again. The chafing banter quickly dying away with the effort. Fording the Red Burn, the way becoming rougher and steeper still. Mountain proper now. And a track which zig zags crazily first left then right. Over and over until the path forks. One way heading left, the other nearly straight ahead. In the lead and take the latter. Urgent shout from Saul bringing up the rear. "Stop." He's got the map in his hand. Gesticulating with his left arm. Turning back hear him say "Not that way. According to this it goes up to Five Finger Gully. No good for us. We go left here."

"You're the boss." Alex grins. "Up to the point when you get between me and my next beer anyway."

I'm saving my breath. Just trudge wordlessly after them. Breathing okay now but not much to spare. The better news is that my legs feel fine and I'm not grumbling about my knees like Steve's been for the last hour. The army crew, moving fast, choose this moment to come past us, heading back down the mountain. Yomping. If that means doing it at twice the speed of a normal human being.

But now I'm mulling over every puzzling aspect of how things are with Alicia. How she responds to me. Why she hides stuff. What she's capable of giving and being. Where she is at this very minute. I'd stop and send her a text right now if I thought I'd get a signal here for my mobile. Miss her with a crunching sickness inside me. And that doesn't make sense. I'll be away from her for a weekend. No longer. Hardly an unbearable lifetime. But something inside me is taking all the elements of our time together and reassembling them in differing orders. Measuring them against unconscious criteria. Pattern recognition. Throwing out answers I can't read. And the symptoms of all this mental activity? Just rising panic. Certainly takes my mind off climbing.

"You ok?" Alex playing minder instead of Saul.

"Yeah. Thanks Alex. Need another drink." Dry mouth. Unclip the tube and bring it to my lips. Take a huge swig of the isotonic mixture. Run it round with my tongue. Swallow and repeat.

"Better?"

"Indeed. Press on." Fall back into step behind Alex and Saul. Steve is scouting way up ahead. Not going to try to catch him. He can slow down and wait for us.

Another easier stretch and cairns begin to appear, strung out along the path. Presumably to help define the route for hikers on more wintery days. To underline our better fortune to be climbing the mountain in June, sporadic patches of settled snow appear and although sweating with effort, I'm glad to be wearing my fleece. Brief pause for a sip of liquid, kicking the mud off my boots against the edging rocks. In a bit the path plateaus out and finally we're almost there. Peering over the edge of a steep drop to our left.

"Gardyloo Gully." Our map reader. "Pretty odd name."

This one I know. "From the medieval French. Used as a warning shout when flinging buckets of night soil out of the window into the street. Gardez-leau!"

"Night soil?"

"Piss and shit to me and thee."

"Very nice."

"Long before Thomas Crapper invented his toilet."

"If he did."

"Well whoever did."

Saul intervenes. "Stop time-wasting. Come on."

A cluster of cairns and we dog-leg around precipitous drops to the summit itself. The red t-shirt gang are already there. Around another cairn. This one a large pile of well-tended stones with a plaque for peace and Burt Bissell, whoever he might be. No time for pondering. Let alone a rest. Quick group photo, a bit of chocolate and we're gone. Saul grinning like a loon. "Bloody good so far. Two hours fifty-five. Minutes ahead of schedule. Keep it up and let's get a shift on."

Down we go. Retracing our steps. Oddly enough in some ways tougher work. Harder on our knees anyway. Too easy to hyper-extend and stumble. Learning the art of turning our feet outwards. Duck-like. And relying on planting the walking poles firmly to take some of our weight. For balance. Early on Alex trips and falls flat on his face amid a volley of curses which tell the rest of us he's not too badly damaged. Haul him onto his feet. An object lesson in pushing ourselves too hard. Get sane. Especially as the light fades.

Halfway down remove our fleeces. The wind's died away and it's much warmer. Or feels it. Probably illusory but we're not checking the actual air temperature. Don't stop and it's not long after nine o'clock before the Ben Nevis Inn heaves into view. When tragedy strikes for one of us. Just carelessness I guess. Steve turning his ankle on flat ground when we're nearly done. And sitting down sharply with a gasp of pain. And team unity kicks in. We are not letting this stop the rest of us completing this challenge. Pick him up bodily. He weighs a bit. But carry him the last hundred yards through the gate and over to our car. Where Matt's fast asleep behind the wheel. Waking as we bundle Steve into the front passenger seat.

"What's up?"

"Bloody idiot's done his ankle."

"We need to get him to the hospital then?"

Exchange looks with Saul and Alex. Say it for all of us. "Hell no. Even if he's broken his leg, he'll have to wait. We're hitting the road."

"Stretches first." Saul being sensible. But he's right. If we don't we'll be seized up by the time we have to start again. Do five minutes. Each calf and hamstrings. Thoroughly. Don't stint.

"What about food?" Alex's stomach speaking for him.

"On the back seat."

He opens the blue insulated bag. Wrapped in foil are a number of cardboard containers. Massive burgers. Stacks of chips. "Matt, you're a bloody marvel. Never been so pleased to see junk food in my life." Grab a burger and get my teeth into it. Tastes wonderful.

"There's a flask of coffee in there too and disposable cups. Help yourselves and then I'll get underway."

Saul passes Steve a burger. "Take your mind off things." I'd laugh but my mouth's too full for that. Realise not even thought about my strapped ribs. Wonderful thing an adrenalin rush.

Twenty past nine and barrelling down the road uttering prayers of thanks to Ronald MacDonald and the good lord who invented him. And telling Steve "Put a sock in it you daft bugger" whenever the jolting fetches a groan out of him. Not much sympathy apparent. We've only done one mountain and we're already a man down. All thoughts are on Scafell Pike.

Shift onto the back seat of Matt's borrowed Chrysler Voyager to try a bit of self-massage on my aching thighs. Easier with my lightweight walking trousers around my ankles.

Ribald comments from the front. "Fucking hell. What you up to?"

"Love the pants!"

Matt joins in from the driver's seat. "What colour are they?"

"Blue and white."

"Not a Lincoln fan then."

"You doing mine next?"

"Bugger off." All in the best possible humour.

Saul and Alex end up sleeping after a fashion. Slumped down as Matt takes the smooth motorway bends at speeds rather in excess of the regulation pace. I can't even snooze. Nor it appears can Steve. But then he's in pain. Quick refuelling stop at a service station. Check my mobile phone. No messages. Try ringing Alicia but no luck. No answer. It's very late. She must be in bed by now. Doze off in the end.

Wake with a start as the car encounters rougher ground. "We're here. Wasdale. Rather you lot than me now." Matt points up at the thick mass of steeply sloping hillside before us. Scafell Pike. And it's five past three in the morning.

Sunrise isn't due until around 4.30 but it's no longer pitch dark. The sky is lightening already. We'll soon be able to see where we're treading. Refill the camel-backs from the massive plastic drum in the back. Restock on emergency rations. Open Matt's big metal cool box and help ourselves to packs of fresher sandwiches than the ones we didn't consume on Ben Nevis. Enjoy the luxury of another swift coffee. There's half a cup each left in the flask for Saul, Alex and me. Matt and Steve can drive off and find their own when we're out of sight. We're still ahead of schedule and intend to stay that way so we don't spend long on the drinks. Find our head torches, get to our aching feet and start doing it all over again. Climbing stiffly but moving quickly nonetheless. Nobody complaining. We can do this.

It's a much harder start than Ben Nevis and as before it takes me awhile to get a proper breathing rhythm going. Hate the feel of gasping for air and burning lungs but it passes. Following Lingmell Gill, a little stream that's probably more of a torrent in the rainy seasons, and clambering up the path over Brown Tongue to Hollow Stones. Nobody speaks let alone jokes. We trudge zombified. Don't even comment as the sun comes up over the horizon. Too deep in personal misery. An even harder patch. Sweating now. Fleece off to climb on half-dressed. The air's good on my skin, particularly when I lift my t-shirt to let it cool my overheated skin. Raising goose bumps. Welcome evidence I'm alive and not actually in purgatory. Take a left fork in the path up to Lingmell Coll and it starts getting easier to my intense relief. Even the last half an hour or so it takes to make it up to the summit. It's well after five in the morning. And we stand there on the top for a short break almost oblivious to the three other teams up there with us. I do notice that the army team isn't one of them. Long gone I presume. Or travelling by helicopter.

The sky is gloriously clear but we're too exhausted to appreciate it. And we have to get safely off this bloody hill with all necessary haste and get prepared mentally and physically to do it all again in Wales in a few hours time. Who's bloody daft idea was this anyway?

As before it's worse than you'd imagine going down the mountain. Everybody's knees are protesting. Heavily reliant on the poles for stability and support. Saul checks his watch obsessively as we go. Ticking off the minutes for us. So I'm in no doubt that I've endured exactly one hour and forty-two minutes of miserably painful walking to get back to the car. And if the thought of the summit got us up, the lure of the car and the food and drink it contains doesn't have the same pull now because getting there only means the necessity of repeating the agony on Snowdon is that much nearer.

Driving. Dozing. Swearing at the traffic.

Pen Y Pass a bit before midday. Under pressure now. Just over four hours to get up and down this blasted third mountain and come in under the twenty-four hour target. And now we're really running on empty. Plodding. Slipping. Suffering. Up the aptly named Pyg Track. No cloud. No rain. But the fine weather means it's a human obstacle course. Plough on past the Sunday strollers, sight-seeing with their families, their children and, in some cases, their pets. Having to almost shove past loiterers on the rocky stairways. Nodding greetings to a few familiar faces from teams we've seen before, going up or down in one of the three countries we've visited in the last day. A dog snaps at my heel as I brush past his skinhead owner. Neither of us apologises to the other. Glares are the order of the day.

We need to make time so it's the steeper but shorter ascent we take and there's no time to dally on the summit. If we could we'd run down again. Luckily too weary for suicide tactics. Stick together and try to gee each other onwards. To speed up as much as it's safe to do so. And the car park comes into sight with six whole minutes to spare. Unbelievable emotion. Would cry if I had the energy. Find myself slumped down beside our car. Touching the tyre. Can't quite believe it's not a mirage. That we made it. That it's done and over and now I'm never going to stand up ever again. It all seems unreal. The sky over me is blurred and drained of colour. I can't hear clearly. Can't even think about how hungry I am. How drained. Almost completely out of it until a single thought shatters the cocooning weariness.

Where's Alicia?

CHAPTER XI: JUNE TO JULY

The women spill out of two cars parked beside ours. Jess hugs Saul for all she's worth. He looks close to collapse. Like I feel. Though he's still on his feet. Alex is holding his wife too. Other people are embracing indiscriminately. But of Alicia; no sign at all.

Can't believe she's not here. She knows how hard we've trained. How much we've invested in this. How tough it will have been. And she's not come. Jess detaches herself and takes the two steps across to me. Crouches down to put her arms around me. Squeezes. Says "I'm sorry. We did go to pick her up. But she wasn't there. We tried ringing her mobile. We waited for her but she never came. And then we just had to set out. Or we'd have been late."

Can't speak. Biting my lip. To hold back the tears which are threatening to spill out. Let her go. Lever myself up onto my feet and walk away. To collect myself. Trying to calm down. Get my ragged breathing under control. Concentrate on my aching leg muscles. Keep moving. It'd be so easy to slump down on a rock and let it all burst out. Except that I'd seize up and never move again. Grit my teeth and force myself into a routine of stretches. For each calf and the hamstrings. Each leg in turn. Holding onto the side of our Chrysler. A monotonous series of movements. Anything other than think. Except it doesn't work. How could it? Keep doing it. And with the weariness comes something closer to calm. And my thoughts slip sideways in a completely different direction. away from self and my sense of loss and hurt towards another awful possibility. That something's happened to her. After all, she'd be here if she could. Wouldn't she?

***

Celebrations are muted. Even after Steve gets back from Accident and Emergency with a copiously bandaged foot and confirmation that he hasn't broken anything. Trying too hard to join in but not really there. Mind you several of the others are flagging. Not the girls or Matt but the rest of us. Sheer exhaustion dragging us down. We've been awake for something close to

148

thirty-six hours. Snoozes in the car between mountains don't count. That's not proper sleep. We're drained of energy. And hungry but too tired to eat much. Or drink alcohol. An hour in and most of us still have something left of our first pints of beer in the glasses in front of us.

Don't want to be the one to start the exodus so intensely glad when Saul stands up and says it for all of us. "This has been an amazing day and I wouldn't have missed it for the world. We made an awesome team. But now really sorry to say I need to go to bed. You can all carry on but I'm crashing right now."

That starts the rot. Twenty minutes later I'm heading upstairs with the rest of the climbers, leaving a much reduced party winding down behind us.

***

The smell of fried eggs in the morning makes me mildly nauseous. But need to force something down me. Settle for bacon rashers stuffed between two doorstops of crusty bread. And coffee. Lots of coffee. Black. Well-sugared.

There are no messages on my mobile. Try Alicia's number. It rings but isn't answered.

The others are less subdued today. Plans are being made. For shopping. For lunch. For a leisurely meander home this afternoon. Who's going where? Who's travelling back when? And with whom?

Matt has to be back in Lincoln by four o'clock whatever. Which is a boon for me. Don't have to wait around. I can go back with all the gear.

Goodbyes are hard. Been through such a lot this weekend. There's a closeness. A bond which wasn't there through training and which nobody wants to see broken up. Still do it though. With promises to meet up for a drink during the week. Hit the road home.

***

149

My house is silent and empty. Still, stale air undisturbed for a long time. Since I left. Alicia's current house is empty too. Locked up securely. No response to repeated knocking. No lights. Not even the builders in residence. Didn't have any great hope of her being there anyway. She doesn't keep much of her personal stuff there anymore and the place may be coming together but it's still primarily a building site undergoing transition into...something else. Try to talk to her neighbours but they seem wary. Don't want to get involved. Tell me nothing.

Should have started by checking to see what's gone from mine. Brain not functioning too well. In fact there's precious little missing. Her expensive hold-all and a small selection of clothes and shoes. Plus her favourite jacket. So she's gone somewhere. Not expecting to be gone too long. But where?

Could go into the office if I want to. It's only mid-afternoon. Where will that get me though? Ring Jane for any news she thinks is worth communicating over the phone now. Nothing urgent. Don't mention Alicia. She'll know soon enough. Try ringing everyone on the short list created in my head of anyone she might confide in. Nobody knows and the best option, her cousin, isn't taking calls.

Sit at home in the gathering gloom and think. Doesn't do me much good. Constructive thought relies on data and there's little of that to fuel any leap of intuition. Don't even know when she left except that it had to be after Friday when I was picked up to go to Oban and before Sunday morning when the girls called for her, setting off to meet us at Snowdon.

Try ringing Janice again. Her cousin. She still isn't answering.

So getting nowhere. Except back to work Tuesday morning. If you can call what I'm doing work. What it really is can only accurately be described as sitting pointlessly in my office avoiding everybody. Alternating between panic-stricken and pondering. Fuelled by a regular flow of coffees. Making my head buzz and keeping me from nodding off but that's all.

Jane tackles me early on. From standing start to complete picture in three questions. "How did the challenge go? Did you finish it? Are you alright?"

"Yes." Catch-all answer. Actually my legs are like boards, I can't bear to stand up and sitting isn't a massive improvement. And without the adrenalin, my side aches abominably.

"Shall I start collecting the sponsorship money?"

"If you would. Thank you."

"What's wrong?"

"Now there's the rub."

"So tell me." Sits herself down across the desk from me. Without waiting to be invited.

"The climbs were fine. Wearying of course. But we got off Snowdon inside the twenty-four hour deadline. So we did it. We aced the challenge."

"And..."

"The girls were there to meet us. As arranged. But Alicia wasn't."

"Where was she?"

"Don't know. She's gone. Disappeared. packed a bag and upped sticks."

"You mean gone for good? Packed everything?"

"No. Just a travel bag. Essentials. You know the stuff." Force a smile. "Hair products. Shoes. Make-up."

"Any note?"

"No."

"And she's not been in touch with you since?"

"Nope."

"And what are you going to do.?"

I don't know yet."

"I can clear the diary today if you want me too. It's fairly light anyway. I kept it that way 'cause I thought you'd be exhausted. Or would you feel better if it was a more normal council day?"

"Don't want to talk to anybody really."

"Then I'll sort it. Anything else now? More coffee?"

"Please."

The day passes without contact. Text Alicia every hour. No reply. Mooch around the office. Don't even go out for lunch. Jane brings me in a sandwich. Egg mayonnaise and cress. She knows I hate egg and cress. Trying to provoke a reaction. Won't give her the satisfaction. Just give her some cash when she fetches in the next coffee. The full extent of my interactions with the human race.

Can't help one thought running around in my head. Even knowing that some of Alicia's personal stuff is missing from her drawers and the dress rail. Couldn't Darryl Weston be something to do with this? Can't rest if I don't raise it. And the obvious person to talk to is Clare. Ring her. She thinks it's a preposterous notion but promises to look into it anyway. Not reassured. Think she's trying to placate me. "You don't get it. He's been emailing her for months. Threats. Declarations of undying love. And he could easily have known I was going to be away last weekend. There were fund-raising posters all over City Hall. Can you really just rule out the possibility that she's disappeared because of him?"

"No. But as I said, it's unlikely. There's no evidence anything untoward has happened to her."

"You should see the emails he's sent. We've been saving them. And Alicia's laptop hasn't been taken. It's still at my house. I could bring it in."

"Why don't you do that?" Clare's answer seems to me to lack empathy or reassurance. Even if that's her going all professional on me.

***

Awake early. Actually not so much waking as giving up on attempting to sleep. Way too soon to go to work. Put on a dressing gown and make a cup of tea. Leave it to cool on the draining board. Take a cloth and a cleaning spray and do the sink and the work tops. Walk upstairs and check the bathroom. Clean enough. Except for the small smear of bloody toothpaste spittle by the tap. New toothbrush must have scraped my gums last night. Hardly aware of it at the time. My mind was elsewhere. Largely still is.

Get stuff ready for the office. Lay out a fresh suit, tie, clean shirt and belt on the bed. Find the shoes I want to wear. Shiny black wingtips. I like pristine shoes. Take them downstairs. Usually enjoy the routine I've evolved for cleaning them properly. Today just a chore in which I can lose myself.

Open the box containing cleaning materials, brushes and rags. Take out a jar of polish and an old spoon. Scoop out a lump of shoe-black. Turn on a gas ring to gently heat the polish on the spoon, its handle wrapped to protect my hand from the heat. Don't let it sizzle or spit. It melts and the viscous liquid can be spread evenly over the shoe using an old cotton duster. Let it soak in while the process is repeated for its twin. Now take each shoe in turn and rub in careful spirals until the shine comes through, when necessary cutting the polish with a touch of spittle until they gleam. A labour of love. And you don't need to think while you do it. Habit and muscle memory carry you through. It just takes time and today time is just there to be consumed

***

The day at work? Much like yesterday. Jane talks to Alicia's line manager for me but he's as baffled as anyone. All he's had is a brief note of a phone message taken by a junior warning him Alicia's had to go away for a few days on a personal matter.

153

Crunch point after refusing any lunch. Not hungry. No knock. Jane doesn't need to knock. Instead of saying something straight off she slams the door shut behind her. Gets my attention alright. Look up and she's leaning her back against it. Arms folded. And a fierce expression across her face. "It's not my place to say this but nobody else will if I don't. You'll wear a hole in the carpet like this. Trailing back and forth like a caged tiger. You shouldn't be here at all. You ought to be out there looking for her. Neil will understand. Just go and find her. That's what you should be doing. You're a very bright man. If anyone can track her down, you can. And there's nothing here won't wait."

Bit shocked at her outburst to tell the truth. Even if this is what personal assistants are for. To point out the bleeding obvious you've managed to miss. First response a bit pathetic. "Don't know where to start."

She glares at me, demanding a response. Pull myself together. Start again. "Thanks, Jane. You're right of course." Decision made. Just like that. "I'll go now." Not sure where. But I'm going. Any action is better than holing up here a moment longer.

***

Try her cousin for the umpteenth time. And she picks up the phone. It's the first she knows of Alicia being away. "I've been away in the Dales."

"Where would she go? To her parents?" I don't even know where they live. Alicia never talks about them.

"My aunt and uncle've been dead for years."

"Any other relatives? Anywhere else she might have gone?"

"I'll check with my parents. Don't think she'd go there though. And they'd have rung me if she'd turned up distressed. There's nobody else I can think of."

"What about where she grew up? Would she head home?"

A vehemently negative response. "Only in dire extremis." Softens. Her sister was killed in an accident and her mum and dad died years ago. She's got no family to go back there for."

"Supposing we're wrong and she has gone back. Where was home?"

A long way away it seems. The other end of the country. The only lead I've got. Janice may be sure she'd never go there but I've got nothing else so that's where I'm going to have to go to start my search for her. Can always do a few on-line checks first. Starting with the regional newspaper. The Western Morning News.

"You haven't asked about Alicia's ex-husband."

"Should I have? Neither of you would talk about him before and I'd rather forgotten he even existed."

"Do you think Alicia's missing of her own accord?"

"Well she packed a bag so it seems she just took off. Why?"

"Because if she didn't, he'd be a prime suspect."

"Why on earth...it's been years hasn't it?"

"It's not too long to harbour a grudge against somebody who tried to kill you. And nearly succeeded."

"I knew something had happened. Didn't know it was that serious."

She tells me. It's not a pretty story. Not the way she remembers it. Nor does it relate to an Alicia I know. Even remotely. Janice's version of events. "He was a complete sod to her. Abusive and violent. And she was completely cowed by him. Hard to understand now. One day he went too far. Got his hands around her throat. Started squeezing. And she fought him. Broke away. Ran into the kitchen. Grabbed a knife and stuck it in him as he came after her. Didn't do a bad job either. Opened a slice clean into him. The evidence was that you could see straight into his chest cavity. But she missed his heart. Nicked a lung. He staggered outside. Bleeding like a pig. He'd have died if she hadn't called an ambulance. Charged with attempted murder. Never tried though. Not fit to stand trial. Or not in the public interest. Or self-defence. Take your pick."

"Which gets us exactly where?"

"Hopefully nowhere. He's probably long gone. Found some other poor deluded little bitch to latch onto. So no...I don't think it's very likely that he's turned up out of the blue and is part of this...But you had to know. In case."

"Thank you. Very helpful." Didn't mean to sound so sarcastic. Just what worry does to you. And fear.

And something Alicia said a long time ago when we were talking about exercise nags at me. "The only time I run is when I'm being chased." There's a double meaning there I didn't see until now. She really isn't the sort to run away from things. So what's driving her now? Who's chasing and more vitally where would she go to hide?

***

"Hello. Can I sit down?"

I'm sitting brooding in a coffee shop waiting for a call from Patrick. The girl who accosts me has the bruised look that some young blondes deliberately cultivate. A pale complexion. A touch of brownish blusher on the cheeks for contrast. Shadows beneath the eyes. A look which only works because it suggests the need for care and sympathy. Non-sexual in its way. Except for those who delight in preying on the vulnerable.

Don't answer her question. Leave her standing. "What do you want?" That came out ruder than intended.

Her response is oblique to say the least. "Are you who I think you are?"

"I might be. Who are you?"

"I'm Sophie. I think she's with my boyfriend."

Making me sit up violently, slopping my coffee and taking notice. "Say that again?

She does. I didn't mishear her first time out. "Is it okay to join you?"

"Yes." Said with a degree of wariness.

"Did you know Alicia's been seeing Darryl again?"

How to respond to that? With the truth? That he's been pursuing her for months. Cyber-stalking. Emailing. Physical harassment. "What do you mean...seeing?"

"That they've been seeing each other regularly. Do you know where she is at the moment?"

"No." Suddenly uncertain that I do want to know after all.

"She's with him."

"Are you sure about that?" Don't want her to be.

"Yes. He told me himself. Said he was going to pick her up and they were going away for the weekend to sort things out."

"He was lying to you. Or he's taken her. Forced her to go with him."

"Don't think he has." An edge in her voice now. Close to anger or hysteria.

"If it's true, where would they go? And it's the middle of the week now."

"He said to the sea. As far away as possible. The West Country."

"Where she spent her childhood. Where I'm heading."

"Take me too. I want to come."

"I don't think so."

"Please. If we find them, I can talk to him. Talk some sense into him. You won't be able to. He hates you."

"I'll think about it. I've got some stuff to do and then I'm leaving in the morning. Give me a number where I can reach you. But I'm not promising."

She gives me her mobile number. "I always carry it. Wherever I go." Of course she does. Don't all the kids? I key the number straight into my phone.

"I'll ring you then."

She gets up awkwardly. Flexes one leg back and forth until it'll bear her weight. Cramp. She must've been sitting on it.

"Please..."

I nod.

***

Patrick's a mine of sporadically useful information. And on this occasion provides a real gem. The name of a man who owes him a favour and can, if he chooses, help me. Even though he lives in Spain. His name's Maxim. I phone him straightaway and get him first time. Yawning thickly but large as life. So far as one can tell across the telecommunications ether. The Austrian accent strong but his English immaculate. Way better than my German anyway.

"You know what I do then?"

"Patrick told me but I don't really know how you find people."

"I work as a tracing agent, I have every database under the sun and what I sell is my skill in interrogating all those sources of information to find people who might not want their business known to the world. So what have you got for me?"

A tough one, I'd guess. It goes back thirty years or more. I'm looking for my girlfriend's family."

"And you can't just ask her?"

"No. She's taken herself off who knows where. It's all a mess." Give Maxim her name and such details as I've gleaned from Janice or the very few things she's ever said about her childhood. Not much. Probably nowhere near enough. But at least it includes the name of the Cornish village of her birth.

"I'm on it for you. Give me your phone numbers and email address and I'll be in touch as soon as I've found anything. Want to know my charges now?"

"No point. I need you. And best to text me. I'm going to be on the road for a bit. Doing a bit of hunting on the ground."

"Right. Good luck then."

A thought. Something I should have mentioned at the outset. "Alicia was married. Years ago but I don't know when. And at the end she stabbed him. He didn't die. No prosecution."

"That opens up police sources as an avenue. What was his name?"

"I don't know. But Valency is her family name not his. I should have checked with her cousin. Supposing I leave her contact details so you can talk to her. I'll text her to say you may be ringing."

"Good thought. And be lucky on your journey."

"Thank you, Maxim."

God knows what using him is going to cost me. Hope he's worth it.

***

Packing when there's a knock at the door. Open it to find Janice on the step. Bringing a sudden burst of hope. "Any news of Alicia?"

"Sorry no." Dashed immediately. "I came to see if you'd heard anything."

"Come in. Cup of tea? Or something stronger?"

"Please. Coffee I think. That man Maxim rang me a bit ago."

"That's good. Could you help him?"

"Not enough, I'm afraid."

Through to the kitchen. There on the breakfast bar, in a plain earthenware pot, the little tree Alicia planted and nurtured, watering and feeding it so carefully, is coming into blossom. With small pale purplish flowers.

"That's pretty. You know what it is?"

"No. I'm no gardener. Sadly."

So she tells me.

What she can't give me is anything useful which might help me find Alicia. Where she would run to if she can't go home.

Back into the kitchen's warmth. Sun streaming in from the back garden. And the little plant in its understated container. It came from a cutting Alicia took in Istanbul and smuggled home, wrapped in damp cotton wool in her hand luggage. The woman who never asked me to love her. Not in words anyway. Only to trust her. When it seems she couldn't be trusted. Growing in my own house. A miniature Judas Tree.

CHAPTER XII: EARLY JULY

Trance music. Alicia's love. Used as a backdrop to everything she does. If she could get away with playing it in the office while she worked, she certainly would. Not my cup of tea really and enforced acquaintance with it doesn't help me relate to the Lemon Jelly compilation disc which starts playing instead of the radio when I turn the car engine over. Must have hit the wrong button. Switch it off. Need to think as I drive. Sophie in the passenger seat doesn't let me. She can't help it. Has to keep talking.

"Do you think we'll find them in this village?"

"I hope so... Because I don't know where else to look. Suppose we could travel round Newquay and St Ives but realistically if they haven't gone to some relative, we'd struggle to find them. They're several days ahead of us and it's a big county. And that assumes he didn't say Devon and Cornwall to put you off the scent."

"He wouldn't lie to me."

"No? Hasn't he been lying to you throughout? Did you know how much he was emailing her? Did you know she'd threatened him with solicitors and the police? Don't suppose he told you any of that."

She flares up immediately. "And don't suppose she told you how she was chasing after him."

"Is that what he said?"

"That's fact."

"Oh yeah. What's the evidence for that?"

"She kept on giving him money for starters."

"He was working for her."

"Even when he wasn't?"

Cold thought. "I think he was blackmailing her emotionally. Just suppose he was extorting money from her too."

"How could he have done that?"

"He must have had something on her."

Sophie demurs and lapses into uncharacteristic silence. Can almost hear the cogs whirring in her head. After a moment she adds something more. "It was quite a lot of money. He left his savings book around once."

"How much are we talking about?"

"A few thousand pounds. And he never earned that in his life."

Ouch. More building blocks for a case I don't want to make. The one against Alicia.

And something else occurs to me I can't share with her. The last time someone backed Alicia Valency into a corner the outcome wasn't pretty. Not for the man involved anyway. Her ex-husband. And if Darryl is forcing her to do anything against her will, I wouldn't give a fig for his continued well-being.

Make it to Exeter services before we have to stop. Desperate for both the toilet and a drink. Coffee not alcohol. And for me a glass of sparkling water with ice and a slice of lemon. Slightly odd on my tongue. As though the lemon was cut with a knife previously used to slice an onion. That's what it tastes like to me anyway. Suppose we could have dropped in on mum but that would have meant explanations I'm not prepared to give.

A light on my mobile flashes, alerting me to a missed call. Maxim. Call him back. "Hello. Found something that might interest you. It's a brief newspaper report from June 1985. About a fatal RTA. Sorry. Jargon's a habit. A road traffic accident. The victim's name is given as Valency. Could be a relative. Says she lived at..." And reads me the address. In the village where I'm already heading. Somewhere specific to look now.

"She lost her sister in an accident many years ago. Know that from her cousin."

"And did you know she's got CCJs. Several of them. I checked County Court records. Judgements for sums in the thousands. She's not financially healthy. Owes maybe a total of thirty thousand pounds sterling. Do you have a laptop with you?"

"My iPad."

"I'll email copies, then."

Seem to be thanking him quite a lot today.

***

End up weary as hell in a Travelodge near St Austell. Enough said. Lie down for a bit. In separate rooms. Worth the extra to get some peace and quiet. I crack first though and go and knock on her door to suggest dining out. Getting hungry and there's nothing remotely healthy in the vending machines in the lobby.

Find ourselves sitting in a very modern and largely empty wine bar in town. Sophie's taken the trouble to dress up. In a short dress and clumpy black boots. She could pass for my daughter. Or I could be taken for her father. Something which doesn't make me feel any more comfortable around her. Beginning to regret yielding to the pressure to bring her with me.

Try to get her to talk about things that don't matter. Pitching for the light-hearted. And doomed to failure. There's only one subject that matters to her. Especially after three rum and cokes.

"I really love him you know. And we've been together for ages. And he really loves me too. It's just... She's turned his head."

I want to slap some sense into her noddle. But that's not my prerogative. Even if she's making me play adult to her child in the psychodrama of her current life.

Content myself with a single hint of incredulity. "Maybe."

"No. It's true. We're going to get married."

"Has he asked you?"

"Not quite."

"Oh."

Can't keep up such a senseless conversation. Nor does gazing round the bar suggest much by way of alternative.

"Drink up. Let's go."

Get mournfully submissive agreement. She's as lost in all this as I am.

***

Destination. A small village deep in the heart of china clay country. Overgrown spoil tips lend the whole area an uncared-for appearance. The occasional well-maintained cottage or over-tended garden only reinforces the general impression of increasing abandonment. The person standing next to us is tall but stooped. Looking his age. Face care-worn despite the smile greeting me. Not the vital and strong man he must have once been. Thirty years ago.

"This has always been a busy road." Two cars race past in quick succession, underlining his point. "It looked different back then." Gestures to the far side of the road. "That wasn't a depot then. Just a field with a gate. By the culvert. Look, there where the stream goes underground." Turns to indicate the hill climbing away to our left. "No verge there either. Just more hedge and some trees. You couldn't see traffic before it came round the bend. And the corner was tighter. They changed the line of the road a bit too. Afterwards."

"They came down the hill then?"

Nods. "Not speeding. But fast enough. It was just a tragic accident. Nobody's fault really. Do you want to go down to the church now?"

"Please."

It's no more than a momentary stroll. Strange to realise this little girl, Alicia's sister, lived her life and died all within the space of a few yards. Her cottage. The road. The gate. The site of the accident. Her grave. Such a short distance between life and eternal rest.

Her memorial is poignant. A small winged cherub on a bed of stone chippings held in place by marble strips. The child's name is engraved in the Cornish fashion along the edging. Clearly visible from the path as you approach. Peer closer, struck by something odd. A misspelling. Comment on it.

"No. That's deliberate. She had the slightest of speech impediments. She couldn't quite pronounce her own name. So they carved it the way she used to say it. Emlee."

Pass round to the foot of the adjacent grave. Sophie hard on my heels. The rest of the story. A larger plot with a black marble headstone. The dates tell you everything you need to know. Emily's father didn't survive her by very many years and her mother lingered barely another five. Beneath their names and dates the legend says only one word. 'Reunited.' Nothing else.

Can see tears starting in Sophie's eyes. Oddly that steels me. Put a hand on her shoulder. Surprised at how slightly built she is. "It's okay."

"But it's so sad."

"Ancient history. Most of the people involved are long gone."

But she puts her finger on the nub of it. "Not Alicia." And she's right.

The man called Trevelyan precedes us out of the churchyard. Pauses at the loosely swinging gate to let us catch up. Adds more details. "First of May. Milk and Cream Day. A school holiday back then. First picnics of the year. Celebrating spring." Hefty sigh. "She was in my class of course. I picked her up off the road. Took her into my house. Said I'd phone the ambulance. But I knew she was already gone. Just didn't want Ivy to see her like that. No mother should have to see her own flesh and blood the way she was...I cleaned her face. She was in an awful state. When I came out...I think she must have known deep down that her little girl must be already dead. She was over there... Sitting in the hedge comforting the biker. He was okay. Just bruises...and shock. He had blood all over the visor of his helmet. I remember that particularly. Seeing it sat by the roadside. After he took it off. He was crying. A big man and he couldn't stop.

"And where was Alicia?"

"I don't know. Didn't see her till much later. When she came home and her mum met her at the gate. Told her then I suppose."

Shiver despite the sunshine. Can picture only too clearly the thirteen year old face of the woman I love. Alicia's stillness. The serious look I know so well. A baffled obstinacy settling in her soul. Forbidding herself tears. Succeeding. All these years.

Shake the proffered hand. Realise Trevelyan hasn't made the obvious enquiries. As though he already senses the nature of my burden. Understands why I'm having to do this.

"Has Alicia been here this week?"

"She's never been back as far as I know." Accompanied by emphatic head movements. "I wish you luck." He says it like he really means it.

***

Sit in my car awhile to think. For once Sophie is silent. With one hand stroke my jaw absent-mindedly. Something reassuring about three days growth. The beard's still in the soft phase before it becomes prickly. If I start the car, the only place to go now is back. There is literally nowhere else to look. That I know of. It's done. I know all there is to know. Don't I? Yet I'm not persuaded this is the end of it. What am I still failing to see? To understand? Tired and hang-dog hungry. Alicia could be anywhere. Maxim's come up short so if there is somewhere else to try then I don't know where that might be. Turn the key in the ignition. Very carefully check the mirrors, pop the car into gear, indicate, release the clutch and move away from the kerb.

Heading home again.

What a waste of time!

Too many miles. Up through St Austell, past signs for Charlestown, running hard for Saltash and the Tamar, across the 1961 road bridge, beside Isambard Kingdom Brunel's much earlier effort. Up past Exeter, onto the M5. The long stretch of motorway northward.

With Sophie reflection can only last so long before it has to spill out. Know that much about her already. "She's not nuts is she?"

"What do you mean?" Although I know exactly where she's coming from.

"Well she could feel really bad that her sister died and she didn't. There's a word for it."

"Survivor guilt."

"Is that what they call it?"

"Yes. But I don't think it's that simple."

"It might be. She feels rotten about herself. And her marriage goes wrong. And now she's got Darryl to deal with. And he can really wind people up you know."

I do know. He certainly winds me up. She obviously doesn't know he's driven me into assault. In self-defence. Actually in law I think it's properly defined as battery but... "He'll be alright. She's grown up a lot. Think she was only twenty-two when her marriage imploded." Could bite my tongue off right then and there. Sophie can't be much more than that now. And she thinks she's old enough to make a life-long commitment herself.

***

Stop at services in Gloucestershire. We both check our phones. Nothing for me. Try Maxim. Get his very precise Austrian intonation on the third ring. "Have you found her yet?"

"No."

"Where are you?"

"Strensham Motorway Services. Coming back up from Cornwall."

"I do have the ex-husband for you. He's in Birmingham. I'm emailing his details to you. His name is James Madden."

Very short on other leads to follow and we can be there by half six. So might as well take the bull by the horns while I'm on this side of the country. And actually having Sophie along may make calling in to confront him seem less threatening.

He lives in a large ground floor flat off the Hagley Road. In Edgbaston. Opens the door himself when I knock. And he doesn't look particularly villainous. Nor much as I'd visualised him. Bulky. Not much hair. Polo shirt bulging a little across the midriff. And a broad but puzzled smile.

"Hello. I'm really sorry to trouble you. We wouldn't be bothering you if we could help it. But we need to talk to you about Alicia Valency."

His smile slips a trifle but he just shrugs. "You'd better come in then."

Leads us through a beautiful, parquet-floored hall which opens into a long lounge-dining room running right to the back of the house. Sitting on a leather settee with a pile of newspapers around her is a skinny little brunette. "My wife, Maggie" he says. "She's a journalist. Hence all the papers. And she knows all about this. They've come about Alicia, darling. I'll put the kettle on. Sit down." He indicates the vacant armchairs. "I'll be back in a mo."

Maggie smiles at me too. Surprising given who and what I've come for. She says "Jim always warned me this day would come. That his ex-wife would come out of the woodwork again. But we're glad you're here. He really does need to talk about it. What are you to her?"

"Her partner. We're not married. Not even been together that long." Saying that feels like treachery. How Peter denying Christ must have felt.

"And your friend?" She indicates Sophie.

"Just a friend."

Jim comes back with a tray. Mugs of tea and slices of lemon cake. Puts it down on a low side-table. "Help yourself." Settles down beside his wife. Gets straight to the point. "Is she alright?"

"Shake my head. "No. No, she's not."

"What's she told you about me? Nothing good, I bet."

"She only ever mentioned that she was even married once. And that was really obliquely. All I know came from her cousin."

"Janice? She never liked me. Not that she had much reason to. I won't make any secret of that. I didn't treat Alicia very well. Shouldn't have married her. I was working in the city. Trading. Lots of drink and drugs. Speed mainly. I wasn't a very nice person to know back then. You know she nearly killed me?"

"I do. Yes."

"What you might describe as a wake-up call. I was in hospital a long time. Lost my job. Not much compassion with those guys. Just business. So I sold up. Moved up here. Started my own business. Met Maggie. A completely different life. But I've always wondered what happened to Alicia."

"I was expecting you to hate her for what she did."

"No. I probably deserved it. In hindsight I was glad they didn't prosecute her. Would have been a travesty. And I wasn't in any state to give evidence for a long time. Anyway if you're here asking about her, where is she?"

"That's the thing. I don't know. She left. Ran away. And I think she's in real trouble. I've tried and I can't find her. I've been down to Cornwall where she comes from. And found nothing much. Did you ever meet any of her family?"

He slowly shakes his head. "She never talked about them. I thought she was an orphan or adopted or something. I should've taken more interest. Been a better husband to her." He takes Maggie's hand between his spatulate fingers. Holds it tenderly as though it's the most fragile object in his universe. And they're not putting on an act for me. I'm certain of that. This is how they feel about each other. They radiate the same emotion as the old couple in that Istanbul bar below the Galata Bridge.

"This is a pointless question. I know that now. But I'll ask it anyway. Have you had any recent contact with Alicia at all?"

"I've not seen her from that day to this. Got the divorce papers through my solicitor. Signed them and walked away. Never ever looked for her. I just thought I'd hear something one day. Rather hoped she'd forgive me. Look, will you do something for me? Let us know what happens. When she surfaces. I'll give you my phone number and email address. Want to know she's okay."

"I've already got all your details. Explain about Maxim. Catch Maggie's eye. She obviously understands all you can find out from the right databases. "And yes I will." Wouldn't have foreseen I'd be promising that either.

"Sorry we can't help you more. But as you already know, she keeps everything in her life compartmentalised and she never gives away more than she has to. Think she was born with the need-to-know principle deeply embedded in her soul. You know. What you don't need to know can't hurt her." A revelation. He's right but I'd never realised it till now.

"We'd better go."

"You don't have to." Maggie puts her oar in for the first time. You could stay tonight if you'd like. The twins are having a sleepover with their friends so we've got spare beds if you want them."

"Lovely thought. But I've exhausted all the possible avenues away from Lincoln and I need to be back home in case she turns up there."

They both stand to shake hands. "Good luck." Maggie impulsively gives me a hug. Don't know what I've done to earn that. "We mean it. Take care."

"I will. Thank you."

Out on the road find I'm leaning against my car door. Flabbergasted. I've just witnessed the complete negation of a belief that people don't ever really change. He certainly has. Unless he's the finest actor ever born. Wonder what sort of wife Alicia was to him. I doubt she was easy.

Still a wasted detour though.

***

Coming around Newark and onto the final stretch north. Until the twin towers of the west front of our cathedral come into view on the hill-crest. Smile a little at the thought of the friend visiting for the first time and commenting on the impressive Norman keep just to the west, along the skyline. It is in fact a Victorian water tower. So much for historical reality.

Wind down the window to take a breath of fresh air. Carholme Road is slick with fallen rain. Clean and sparkling as the street lights flicker into life. Pass a group of runners trotting alongside the old race circuit, the unkempt grass notwithstanding. Recognise one or two of them as local footballers. I'm not wrong. Their tops carry the Lincoln Imp.

Drop Sophie off at Darryl's home and wait for her round the corner. She's back in five minutes. "No go." Meaning he's not back yet.

Take her to her own place.

"Promise you'll ring me if you find anything out won't you? You've got my number now?"

"Yes, Sophie. I will."

Before she gets out of the car she asks something that's obviously been bothering her. "What did Alicia do to him? To Jim?"

No dodging that question. "She stabbed him."

Absorbing the answer, she hovers on the pavement holding the car door open. "She wouldn't hurt Darryl...Would she?"

Can't answer that one.

Turn the key in my front door. Push the door open against some resistance. Coats lying on the hall floor. While I've been away, somebody's been in my house.

CHAPTER XIII: THE REST OF JULY

I don't leave the coats on the floor. I'm pedantic about hanging them up on the wall-hooks in the porch. Nothing disturbed in the sitting room. Call out "Alicia." More hope than expectation. No response. And the house retains an empty feel to it.

Into the kitchen. A rinsed mug I didn't use on the draining board. She's been here. Run upstairs. More of her stuff gone from the rail in our bedroom. Down again. Looking for the note she must surely have left for me. But it isn't anywhere. Doesn't exist.

Sink onto the settee. Nothing like falsely raised hope to bring on despair. But on one thing I'm determined. No tears. Pull myself together and do a thorough walk-through, making a mental list of everything she's taken this time. All I can identify are a dress, a couple of tops, some jeans and the main contents of her underwear drawer. The whole lot bundled into one of my old cases.

This tells me that she's alive. That she hasn't moved out, lock, stock and barrel. That she's still only got clothes for days rather than weeks. What it doesn't give me is any clue where she's gone. Or how she is.

A thought strikes. Not checked the bathroom. Her toiletries on the shelf look untouched.

Phone Maxim for a second opinion. "That's all she's got with her. Am I wrong in thinking that implies she doesn't expect to be away that long? You know about these things. What do you think?"

"Largely I agree with you. Although I don't think we can have a clue what's going on in her head. And we're still stuck on the thorny problem of where she actually is." I like his inclusive language. Good that he sees this as a mutual problem. Rather than my imposition upon him as a hired hand.

"When people go missing...How many end up coming back?"

"Irrelevant. She's already bucked the stats. She came back for more clothes. So she's not contemplating doing something stupid."

"You're saying she's not suicidal." It's a thought that's been nagging at me ever since I got off that bloody Welsh mountain.

"No. She's not that. She may not be thinking clearly. But she's got a plan. And there's something very specific she's hiding from."

"You mean me?"

"Don't be a berk. Isn't that what you say? Berk. Where I would say simpleton or idiot. She's got her reasons and they're external. I guarantee you that. This is not about her life with you. It's her past catching up with her. Or...Well we'd be guessing."

"Financial pressures?"

"Could be in part."

"What would you do?"

"Now? She's been back once. She's still got stuff in your house. Does she keep everything at yours?"

"She doesn't really have a home. She sold it to buy the one she's doing up. And that's still a building site. Nearly done and ready for sale maybe. But she wouldn't leave possessions there. What's not at my house is in a storage unit. You know furniture and stuff."

"You should check if she's been back to the unit. They'd have a record. Email me the details and I'll find out for you."

"Okay."

"And you have to stay calm. Sit tight now and wait for news."

"But she's not been in touch at all. No calls. No texts. No note. And there's Darryl..."

"I know. You said. But when she's ready she will. I'm sure of it."

"Thanks, Maxim."

"You're welcome."

Hang up. Not greatly comforted. Just marginally reassured. Try to sleep. Don't manage that very well.

It looms emptily but at least it's the weekend so I don't have to go into the office. I can be here at home if anything materialises.

Hardly dare to even shoot down to the corner shop for essential groceries. Every one of the twenty minutes it takes leaves me sweating with anxiety. This isn't rationality. More like the road to madness. Ollie at the gym would be telling me to stop and breathe deeply in and out for a while. Do just that. And feel calmer for it. Enough to cook myself some lunch. And to eat it. Then lie down to doze on the settee. For an hour or more.

A ringing phone ending all speculation. Fumble for it in the half-light. When did I pull the curtains? Praying it's her.

It's not.

It's Patrick, on the other end. In an official capacity from McFarlane's. "Got a client asking for you. I mean Alicia of course. Can you come now?"

"Right away. Is she with you? She wants me? Where does she want to meet?"

"No choice in the matter. Come to my office and I'll take you to see her."

"Where is she?"

Avoids the question. "Come over as soon as you can." It must be bad news. She's in the hospital. Where else?

"Twenty minutes then."

Make it in twelve. And where we go to is end the waiting area of Lincoln Central Police Station. About as grim a place as could be in the mood I'm in. Because they'll allow Patrick to see Alicia. He's her solicitor. But not me. They won't let me see her. Instead a stern-faced sergeant makes it clear that's he's under instructions to arrest me if I don't agree to answer some questions for them.

***

Sitting opposite a familiar face from the queen in the West and elsewhere. A woman's who's been in my house. Someone who used to be my friend.

"Sorry but I need you on record. This will be an interview under caution. If won't take long. Unless you want a solicitor present."

"Well my solicitor would be Patrick." Which earns me one of Clare's fleeting smiles.

"He's down in the cells with Alicia. But don't suppose we need him. Do we?"

"No."

"Let's get on with it then. We need to use an interview room with recording facilities and a colleague present. Come with me."

Accept that necessity. Nod. Do as I'm told.

The room we end up in looks like it's been modelled by reference to a set from a poor television crime series. In other words it's what you'd expect. Basic. Functional. Uncomfortable.

Introductions are made for the benefit of the cameras. Present Chief Superintendent James, Detective Inspector Burton and me. Rights are read out and waived. The interview starts. And pretty quickly I'm in unexpected territory. Deep water. And entirely baffled. I'd thought we'd be dealing with Alicia's disappearance but what's coming at me is something else entirely. Neutral questions give way to things I don't think I know anything about at all.

"Tell me about your dealings with the K&S Design Partnership."

The truth on this one's easy to state but it's relevance to me is unknowable. "There aren't any. I don't know them."

"You've never had them do any work for you?"

"No. Of course not."

Do you know James Keel and Ronald Smith?"

"No." A pregnant pause and something occurs to me. "There's a James Keel who works for the council. I've seen his name on emails. I'm pretty sure I've never actually met him."

"And Ronald Smith?"

"Never heard the name till now."

Clare opens a manila folder and pushes some papers across the formica table to me. "Take a look at these."

The letterhead is crisply professional. A stylised star and the name of the company. The one they were asking about a few moments ago.

"Have you seen these estimates before?"

Leaf through them. Costings for building work. Various dates over the last three years. Made out to another company. More Building Developments Limited.

"No."

"Look carefully at the properties they relate to."

Shuffle and check. One address stands out. Colenso Terrace. Then another. A town house on the edge of the West End.

"Do you recognise any of them?"

Sigh. "Yes I do."

"Which ones?"

Tell them.

"Do you know who owns them?"

Have to drag up the name from a very deep place down inside me. "Alicia did. She sold them."

"For the record you're referring to Alicia Valency?"

Nod.

"Please speak up for the tape."

"Yes."

"And you're sure you've never seen these documents before?"

A leading question. And a closed one. Clear what answer Clare expects to be repeated but does she know it's the truth?

"Yes." Clarify my response. "I've never seen them before today."

"Will you sign a statement to that effect?"

Slightest hesitation but no real choice. "I will."

"This interview is terminated at..." She checks her watch and adds the time. Presses a couple of switches.

The Inspector stands up. "Are we done, boss?"

"We are, Mike. I just need another minute here."

Michael Burton lets the door close softly behind him.

Clare leans across the table. "You don't really know what's happening here, do you?"

"Is it that obvious?" Shake my head in the clearest denial I can make.

"Those estimates are for building work purportedly to be carried out for and by Alicia. They were logged in the council's files. Attached to applications for improvement grants. If that's what they're still called. Which were paid in due course to Alicia. Some of the work may be completely fictitious. Some of it was unquestionably carried out. Inspections were made before payments were approved but there may have been somebody in the Building Control service who was in on it. Although they weren't all inspected by the same individual. Could even be a link to the Lenahan case and the planning officers who went down."

Slow to dawn. But only one conclusion to be drawn. "This is a real crime. A fraud."

"Sadly it is."

"But if you can't show payments were made for non-existent works, where's the proof? Of any fraud."

"She paid a colleague in the grants set-up to cook up costings at the top end of the appropriate scale. Tolerances, they call them. They ended up in the estimates from K&S and the claims made by Alicia supported by inflated builders' invoices from a company she set up herself. So maximum grant income for minimal outlay."

"But the grants would have had to be repaid when the houses were sold."

"True. But the houses weren't sold."

"There were estate agents boards..."

"Just a front. She rented them out. And you didn't know and you didn't take any share of the profits. Did you?"

"No. I didn't know any of this.""

She puts a hand on my shoulder. Clearly she believes me.

"I wanted to talk to you before but first I had to be sure you weren't knowingly involved in this."

"And now you know..."

"Yes. I do. And I'm sorry."

Shrug. Her expressed sorrow doesn't change anything much.

"What will you do now?"

"Resign."

"You don't have to do that."

"Yes I do. There's not much credibility in having a relationship with a member of staff who turns out to be defrauding the council. It raises a massive question over my judgement. Not survivable really."

For a moment she looks like she's going to disagree but the moment passes. She nods her acceptance of my logic. "I suppose so. I enjoyed working with you though."

"Me too. But that's going to be the wrong side of a closed door soon."

"Is there anything I can do?"

Shake my head. "Don't think so. But thanks for the thought. Will Alicia get bail in the morning?"

"Not very likely. It'll be opposed. She's a flight risk. We don't even have her passport so she's hidden that somewhere. Remanded in custody pending trial I suspect. And once again I'm sorry."

"That's it then."

"Fraid so. Look. There is one more thing I ought to tell you. Alicia doesn't know this yet. You handed in her laptop and password to us when she went missing. To look at the email traffic from Darryl Weston. Which we did."

"Yes. So what."

"We also found other stuff when we were going through it. Links to potential evidence of criminal activity."

"You're saying what I did helped put her in here."

"To a point. If she chooses to view it that way."

Shit. "She might very well see it like that."

"Of course we could've got the laptop under a search warrant anyway."

Not much consolation in that argument either. More food for thought. And a decision. An easy one. Time to have a drink. A seriously stiff one.

"Do you want to see Alicia now?"

"Can I?" Alcoholic anaesthesia will have to wait.

"You can."

"Yes please."

"I'll get somebody to take you down."

***

I'm allowed to join her in another interview room. Marginally better than a cell I suppose. Patrick leaves us to it. She looks weary. Drained by the relentless grey colour scheme. She can't even raise a smile for me.

"Where were you? When I was chasing around Cornwall after you." Not going to add in the complication of Sophie's presence. Or what I know about Darryl.

"Don't make me tell you."

"Why ever not?"

"Because you'd be angry."

"When have I ever been angry with you, girl?"

No answer. Just a dropping of her gaze. Let it go nevertheless.

She won't say anything after that. Just clings like she never wants to let go. And of course in the end they make me leave.

It feels a very long walk out onto the street.

CHAPTER XIV: AUGUST TO OCTOBER

Recover Alicia's car. Abandoned near Patrick's office. She went with him and handed herself in apparently. There's no sign of her designer hold-al. In the car's boot there's just my battered old bag. Full of her stuff. Going through it, one surprise. A box of proprietary drugs. No idea what they are until I check on-line. Anti-depressants. Suppose I should have known she was taking them. But you don't do you? You take someone's moods and emotions as being normal for them. Whatever they are. If there's no past history to compare against.

***

Misery. Helplessness. They can make it look so attractive in the movies. Posed against a glorious skyline. In reality it's neither photogenic nor cool. Just grim. The feelings also invariably accompany an ongoing situation which is neither controllable nor resolvable by the efforts of those most affected. If that's too generalised and an over-gloomy point of view, I apologise. But it's how it feels.

There's one other factor in the mix. An urge to take it out on somebody else even if their culpability is no more than marginal. In this case there's an obvious scapegoat in Darryl Weston. Nobody's arrested him. So he gets to pay the price for Alicia's incarceration even if it would have happened irrespective of anything he chose to do or say. Life's cruel that way.

It's a confrontation almost overdue. The boot on the other foot now. Each weekend and every evening after work watching his mother's house to get a handle on Darryl's movements. His routines are in fact predictable as hell. Friday nights on the lash with his mates. Saturday sleeping in and then out with Sophie in the evening, usually going no further than the pub on the corner with a visit to the chippy on the way home. Sundays playing football for a team off St Giles. Weekdays drifting between labouring jobs on various building sites followed by snooker or he's back in the pub. Occasionally he breaks with custom and it's the cinema with Sophie. Sometimes he's with an older dark-haired woman he collects in his old Skooby and later drives home the long way round. Via West Common.

Easy to work out the overlapping times when his mother is also out; her regular bingo nights and her visits to her grown-up daughter, Darryl's sister.

At last nerve up to do what I've been planning. On a dark mid-week evening after both of them have left the house. The task? Breaking and entering. The aim? To repossess the savings book so Darryl can't readily access whatever money he's gained from Alicia. Also to find any papers Darryl might be holding which relate to Alicia's properties. I'd like to be in and out in five minutes. Certainly no longer than fifteen. And that's probably much longer than any professional burglar would choose to be there. But it depends how and where Darryl hides things.

It's become quite obvious to me that the weak point is the back door. If I cover the glass with Blu-tack, one hard tap should give me a hole to reach through and from previous visits I know they're daft enough to leave the key in the lock. Turn it and I'll be in.

Actually it proves much easier than that. Test the handle first and to my surprise they've left the door unlocked.

Be brisk. In and upstairs. No dogs. Heart stops when something shoots past my legs but it's only a cat. It's obvious which room belongs to Darryl. It's a mess. Clothes on the floor and... I could pull everything out and dump it into a heap and no one would know he'd been burgled. I don't. One drawer contains a mass of papers. No time to go through them but the bank book's there. Drop it all into a plastic bag I've been carrying in my pocket. Cursory check of the rest of the house. Haven't quite got the nerve to search the lounge because the big picture window looks out onto the road and the curtains aren't drawn. Get out quick.

Back to the front of the house. Check nobody's walking past. Mooch out as casually as I can manage. Don't look back. Round the corner. Back to the car. And away.

No great outcome from the dose of breaking and entering. True I've got my hands on a savings book showing a current balance in excess of eleven thousand pounds but the rest of the papers were rubbish. Why he'd keep them I couldn't tell you. In disgust post them back through the Weston's letterbox two days later, letting them drop handful after handful onto the doormat. And leave them to wonder who had them and why.

So neither useful evidence nor material for brainwaves. The only link left to exploit is Sophie. Nothing to lose. Ring her.

At least my voice piques her curiosity. "What's happened?"

"Well Alicia's in police custody."

"You mean...? What for?"

"It's complicated but Darryl could well be joining her in there soon. Haven't they pulled him in for questioning yet?" Lay it on thick. "He's in this up to his neck. And I may be the only one who can save him. Can you get him to meet me?"

"Doubt it."

"Then get him into a pub in town. Somewhere quiet without telling him I'm coming. Honestly he needs to talk to me."

"Are you sure? You're not setting him up?"

Where do they get their cynicism? Too much television I suppose. "Course not."

"I'll try. When?"

"Any lunchtime this week. Sooner the better."

"Alright." The obediently submissive tone which seems to be her natural defence in times of trouble.

***

As Sophie promises, they're in The Witch and Wardrobe on the waterfront at one o'clock on Wednesday. Not quiet at all. It's so busy I don't immediately spot them and have to part a sea of student drinkers to reach them. It does mean Darryl can't get away easily although the expression on his face when I heave into view tells me that's exactly what he wants to do.

Sophie puts a hand on his arm. "He's not here to fight." That took courage. Revealing fore-knowledge of my arrival. He shrugs her hand away. Glares at her.

"Okay to sit here?" The miracle of a spare bar stool beside them. He doesn't tell me not to. So I do. No need for preliminaries. "You know where Alicia is? Remanded in custody. Charged with fraud. And you're next if you don't help me."

"Why me? I ain't done nothing." Could point out the effect of a double negative but he's unlikely to appreciate an English lesson at this point. "To start with you're holding the proceeds of crime."

"What d'ya mean?"

Pull the savings book out of my pocket. "Recognise it?"

"Where did you get that? You stole it. You must have."

"Doesn't matter. Where did the money come from? But we know that don't we? And where did Alicia get it?"

Darryl says nothing. But his look is calculating. The wheels spinning in his head right now.

"The safest thing you can do is give it back. If you want me to keep you out of prison."

"I haven't spent none of it."

"I know. Shall we put it back?"

"Now?"

"Yes. Now. We walk down to your bank and transfer the money into my account. I in turn am going to be lodging it with her solicitors." The last bit's a lie. Safe enough. I don't expect him to know the ins and outs of the money laundering regulations. He flicks a look at Sophie. Seeking reassurance. What he should do.

She says "I think you should."

He doesn't argue the toss. Stands and puts his hand out to take the bank book from me. I stick it straight back in my pocket. Safest place for it isn't in his possession. Think he'll say something but he doesn't. Walks out good as gold with Sophie on his heels. And me a pace or two behind her. Up to the city branch of his bank in Guildhall Street. The one which used to have a cashpoint out front but now boasts an actual hole in the wall. Still boarded over despite the passing of the months.

We sort the transaction there and then. And he even stays resolute when the clerk questions the transfer and has to get managerial approval for it.

Afterwards. Still in the foyer he asks "What now?"

"Well you've got rid of the most incriminating evidence. The next thing is the emails you sent. Have you kept copies?"

He nods. Cowed now. Not even denying things in front of Sophie. Obviously frightened. Just where I want him. Give him my card. "Here's my email address. Forward every email you ever sent to or got from her so I can go through them and work out what's incriminating."

"You'd do that for me?"

Not for you, you bloody daft idiot. "Yes. Don't need you as another witness for the prosecution."

"Ok. What else?"

"If I think of anything, I'll ring Sophie. And we'll meet again next week after I've seen the solicitors."

He nods thoughtfully. Completely out of his depth. The second time I've come close to feeling sorry for him. It could get to be a habit.

***

Long conversations with Patrick conducted in either the untidy confines of his office or in the back room of some pub or other. As

186

good a choice of places as any to cook up a defence for the inexcusable. Not much difference between office and pub except in the quality of the alcohol served. The single malt from Patrick's second filing cabinet from the left far superior to anything served where you have to pay for your drinks. And I doubt his bill for legal services will include whisky among the rechargeable disbursements.

I get pre-views of all the evidence revealed by the prosecuting authorities and to understand the compelling nature of all the fingers pointing to Alicia's guilt.

We may not be going great guns at drafting an irresistible defence strategy but involvement in these sessions brings me one other benefit. Regular attendance with Patrick at a local remand centre to see and comfort Alicia. Actually the boot's on the other foot. Now things are out in the open she seems more concerned with how I'm feeling. As though lies could really be a thing of the past.

The prison more closely resembles a zoo than a place in which to house young women still technically innocent of any offence. Not yet tried and found guilty. There are some seriously disturbed people in here and being the ones locked up seems to make many of them feel they have the right to act up for the visitors. Patrick and I get shouted at and worse. On one occasion a passing inmate under escort spits copiously in my direction and her accuracy requires multiple tissues to remove the physical evidence. Less easy to blot it out of my mind though and it leaves me even more nervously discomfited to be there than normal. It won't feel any better until the jacket can go to the dry cleaners.

Alicia needs and gets hugs. And invariably she has a hit list of things she needs which I'm to fetch in next time. Usually toiletries.

Get a still more extensive shopping list after a conference with Alicia and her barrister, Jeremy Hemsley-Robb. Afterwards he strongly suggests planning for the worst. Not a conversation I want to have at all. Hemsley-Robb saying "You need to pack some stuff for her. Just in case. No more than two average sized boxes. The sort they deliver crisps in. Or plastic ones I suppose'd be alright."

"What should I put in? What'll she need? What'll she be allowed to take in with her?"

"Here. Have a piece of paper." He tears a leaf out of one of his spiral-bound notebooks. "And borrow my pen. It'll be a lot easier for her to take it in with her than trying to get it to her later on. And there'll be no visitors for the first month anyway. And you're not family so there's no guarantee even after that...It's going to be tough for you."

"Tougher for her."

"True. Now make the list. Starting with basics. Deodorant and stuff."

"Can she have her mobile?"

"Definitely not allowed. It'd be confiscated immediately. She can earn access to a fixed phone so do her a note of essential phone numbers. None of us ever need to remember them these days? Do we? Is she on any medication?"

"Yes. I've got her tablets."

The barrister nods. "Clothes then. Jeans and tee-shirts. Plenty of underwear. Socks. Does she smoke?"

"No."

"Put in eighty fags. That's the maximum allowed. Better than money in there. And envelopes, stationery, stamps, pens. After that stuff to pass the time. She can take a radio and spare batteries. Books. Things she won't find in the average prison library. Drawing and painting materials are good. Notebooks. That's about it really. She could take a guitar in as well if she wanted."

"She doesn't play."

"Okay. Can't think of anything else."

"Do you actually think she'll go to prison?"

"It's a toss-up. She may well go down. But we'll do our best to prevent that happening. Prayers won't hurt at this stage."

"I'm not the praying kind. But I'll consider starting."

It's not a reassuring conversation to reflect upon. Go home and start boxing up the suggested items with a heavy heart and more than traces of moisture in my eyes.

***

Eventually there's nothing else to discuss with the lawyers. All further preparation rendered redundant because there's a hole in the arguments and mitigation which Alicia won't help us to fill. It's as though being convicted would be infinitely preferable to having to discuss what must be painful family history. Or she can't accept its relevance to her current problems. How do I get it through to her that this isn't peripheral. It's potentially the difference between having a life again and the prospect of any such life being indefinitely deferred or completely scrapped.

Even if she's going to hate me for it I've got no choice but to take a psychological scalpel and slice through all the healed scabs of her defences. Because I've not said a word to anyone so far about what I discovered in Cornwall. Not even to Patrick. Now it has to be done. And damn the consequences.

Not really a conversation best started in a visiting room but needs must. Talking to her across a chipped formica table. "So thirty years ago. Where were you when it happened? The accident."

"How do you know about that?"

"When I was trying to find you in Cornwall. I went to St Stephen. And Foxhole. Janice told me where to go."

"Oh." Said listlessly. Without apparent emotion or relief.

"You have to tell me."

"No. No. I won't. I can't."

Turn up the heat. "This is your last chance. If you don't then I'm going to walk out of that door and you'll never see me again."

"You wouldn't do that. I thought you loved me."

"I do. But I'll leave you just the same."

Give a minute or more. Silence. Stand up. Turn away towards the warders guarding the door and she cracks.

"Please. Don't. I saw it, you know. Saw it all."

Turn back. Finally a breakthrough.

"I thought you were at a friend's house. They said you came back and your mum told you what happened."

Head-shaking denial.

"I was there. I saw her go over the road with her best friend, Maria. She had no business crossing over. They were just going down to the shop for sweets. But there were ponies in the field. I heard her calling them but they wouldn't come and they started to come back across."

Pause and prompt. "So the motorbike hit her."

"No. It didn't happen like that. It came round the corner as they were crossing but they heard it in time and ducked back into the gateway. Then when it passed they started out again. They couldn't hear there was a second bike right behind. Maria broke for the far side of the road but Emlee tried to go back. He swerved but he couldn't steer round both of them. He came off into the hedge. The bike hit the ground and slid down the road. Such a horrible screeching sound. I'll never forget it. I should have gone to her. She was lying there, completely still. I saw Mr Trevelyan come out of his gate...And I ran away. I left her to die.

"You couldn't have done anything for her. She was killed outright."

She gulps for air. "Not the point. She was my little sister"

"You were only a girl yourself."

She shakes her head. Vehement objection.

"And this is what this is all about?" Can't quite see how guilt leads to what she's done. "You're taking the blame for what happened to Emlee."

Denial. "I came to terms with that in the end. But when Mum and Dad died too, I was completely on my own. And I learned to deal with that in time. But I can't be close to someone else. Can't be responsible for anyone except myself. Can't rely on anybody being there for me."

So the money thing is about security. Pure and simple. Say so. The mulish look arrives, lingers a second and is suddenly gone. She closes her eyes. And the word eases from her lips. "Yes." The slightest hesitation. "That's how it is."

Long silence. Eventually feel compelled to break it.

"Do you want some water or something?"

Shake of her head. "Ought to tell you the rest."

"Okay. I'm listening."

"She had a new dressing gown for Christmas. It was scarlet and she loved it. So Mum and Dad buried her in it. With matching slippers. Everyone in the village turned out on the day."

She stops. I'm not going to interrupt. Gaze intently at her face which carries a thousand yard stare. She's so far away, she seems unaware where she is and who she's talking to.

"They had a white cloth to line the sides of the grave. Somebody said she shouldn't have to touch anything that wasn't beautiful. The women from the church spent all morning sewing wild flowers on it. She was buried in a sea of violets. I don't remember much else about the day. It passed in a sort of blur. Not much else worth remembering I suppose."

Prompt her for the first time. "What happened to your father?"

"I really loved him. I wanted him to be so proud of me. But he couldn't get over losing her. I was like a distraction from his grief that he didn't want. She was his favourite. Not serious like me. She was pure mischief and he adored her for it. The last thing she said to me the day she died...She came up and grabbed me. And she said...like she'd only just realised...She said 'Alicia, you've got breasts!' And I said 'You'll have them too in a while, Sweet-pea.' But of course, she never did."

An enormous tear starts to travel down Alicia's tilted cheek. She makes no move to wipe it away. Watch it roll on. Put out a finger to arrest it only as it arrives at the point of her chin.

"Can you die of a broken heart? Because I think he did. And my mum was never the same after he'd gone too." Gulp of pure hurt. "I left at eighteen. Got a job with estate agents in Truro. Didn't go home much after that. Got qualified. Moved away. Got married. All that trouble with Jim. Got divorced. Wound up here." Presume she means Lincoln rather than our immediate surroundings in the remand centre or sitting on a plastic-covered mattress back in her doubtless grubby cell. Where she'll be sitting again in a bit.

***

Never thought I'd be made so familiar with the processes of a criminal trial as I now am. From an insider's very personal and self-interested perspective. Not that it's either long or particularly fascinating; any rehearsal of the evidence was rendered unnecessary weeks ago by the lodging of guilty pleas by all the co-defendants; Alicia and the other two.

The courtroom's narrow and needs a fan or two to make the atmosphere palatable. The jury benches and the witness box are on one side and public seating opposite. Not very far apart, putting everyone cheek by jowl with the lawyers and their supporting cast of assistants in front of the judge. Furthest removed is the dock at the back with the hidden staircase down to the cells.

Thanks to Patrick, I don't have to sit squeezed between reporters from the local media, trial groupies and opportunistic visitors; the modern day equivalent of old ladies knitting beside the guillotine but still sharing all the ancient characteristics of schadenfreude. I'm behind Alicia's legal team with my back hard up against the large wooden box in which she'll be standing in a bit. The only drawback is not being able to see her without twisting my head at a stupidly impossible angle in conjunction with her leaning forward over the dock.

Even though I've not been able to see her this morning, I can picture where she's waiting below. As I'm waiting impatiently now. Restless as the hands on the big wall-clock shift towards and past ten o'clock. Eventually the crashing of a door deep in the bowels of the building heralds movement. Several sets of feet scuffing the stairs. Coming up to see out the final act of this drama. From consideration of social inquiry reports, through pleas in mitigation to sentencing.

A little whisper. "Hi, you." And get a glimpse of her strained face before a prison officers makes her sit down.

Not for long.

"All rise." Stentorian bellow from a black-robed usher announcing the man in the red robe and impressively ancient wig. To whom all bow, receiving a cursory nod in return as he settles his bulk down onto a doubtlessly extravagantly padded and comfortable seat cushion.

Vaguely aware of someone settling into the chair next to mine. A woman. Clare James. A hand on my arm. And a nod of support. "I'm sorry" she says. It's all she ever seems able to say to me these days.

"You were only doing your job." Obviously true but easier to say than to accept, emotionally speaking.

Trying to keep my eyes open as the long mitigation speeches start. I've no interest at all in the arguments in favour of Keel and Smith but Alicia's barrister has obviously drawn the long straw and gets to go last. My head droops onto my chest and then a sudden start drags me bolt upright only for the sagging process to begin all over again. It's in that state of marginal reality that I hear an outcome. Time served and a suspended sentence. Or did he say something about probation for a first offence? Deep-seated relief. No energy left to express anything except weariness, but somehow get onto my feet.

Meet her outside on the steps. Don't know what to say. Settle for hugging her. It's already winter-cold outside. She lets go. Shivering in her light-weight jacket. "Where's the car?"

"Round the corner." Her elbow brushes my arm. Smiling now.

"We'll have to run to keep warm. Last one there's a dork."

Startled I lose precious seconds to her. Heel-kick into urgent motion. Haring down the street after her. Laughing children. The wind takes all that past pain and this cackling glee to its bosom, hugs it there, clutches it in loving fingers and lays it to rest.

But that's only how it is inside my head. I've been drifting in an exhausted daydream. In this over-heated little room. The clock says I've been asleep for almost thirty minutes and finally Hemsley-Robb's on his hind-quarters, doing his best to paint Alicia as a troubled soul with a problematic past and as someone unlikely to pose any future problems to society if left at large.

The judge, a red-faced little man with pock-marked cheeks, appears patently unconvinced. And promptly hands down two year sentences to the other two and then..."As the principal beneficiary...and a public servant...term of imprisonment unavoidable...three years. Take her down."

Hear the little gasp only too plainly. However steeled we might have been before, it's still a horrible shock to hear such a sentence pronounced. Standing, she clutches the rail convulsively and a drop of moisture falls on my forehead. Then another tear. Mingling with my own.

I'm allowed to see her in the cells before the white panel truck comes to take her away. A favour I owe to Clare's personal intervention. We don't say much. Holding onto each other in shock. Eventually she asks me something important. "Will you wait for me?"

Nod. Don't trust my voice right now. I don't know if it's a promise I can keep through the coming shipwreck. Only that I'll have to try.

***

What else is there for me to say or do? I've belongings to pack into boxes; a house to place on the market because I can't pay the mortgage any longer; a few goodbyes to say. Not sure where I'm going but staying in Lincoln, holding on to a few grand in fraudulently obtained funds, isn't an option.

Last stop the Guildhall. A final look around. Pause in the lobby to look at the portrait gallery. Photographs of Town Clerks to the Corporation down the ages. Each wearing the same old black velvet, Victorian gown and a formal barrister's wig. The last picture in the line is mine. In a week or two a second date will be added beneath it. The date on which my tenure as Chief Executive ended. A shame. But there it is.